I0684318

GEORGIANA

By Sue Barr

Published by: Susan L Barr
Print ISBN: 978-1-7770825-1-2
Cover Design by Midnight Muse
Text copyright ©2020 Susan L. Barr
All Rights Reserved

This story would not be possible without the wonderful works of
Jane Austen and her book, Pride & Prejudice

Dearest Rob
You will <u>always</u> be my Mr. Darcy
I love you more than key-lime pie

She longs for true love...

A dowry of thirty thousand pounds places a hefty weight upon the shoulders of Miss Georgiana Darcy. Her tender heart has been broken before by a cad who cared not one whit for who she was, but as a prize to be won, and she fears no man will ever see the worth of her heart.

Duty and honor...

These are the stalwart columns which hold up the life of Maxwell Kerr, Fifth Duke of Adborough. After rescuing Miss Darcy from an inescapable compromise, an offer of marriage is as natural to him as breathing air. When he discovers this is not the first compromise she has evaded, anger becomes his faithful companion and threatens their tenuous bonds of love and respect.

Chapter One

The carriage with its three occupants bumped along the narrow road. At the sound of glass against glass, Georgiana Darcy spared her maid Anna, who clutched a basket of preserves on her lap, a glance. The trail, though rough in some places due to the spring storm which had trundled through Derbyshire last week, had dried out enough so that she could visit some long-term tenants before she left for London. The thought of leaving Pemberley and all that was familiar in order to prepare for her first Season caused her stomach to clench. She knew the fear and shyness was irrational, but the thought of meeting so many new people almost made her sick.

"Are you quite all right, Miss Darcy?"

The polite inquiry came from Lord Nathan, better known as Mr. Kerr to the parishioners of Kympton parish. His curly dark hair, broad shoulders and ready smile caused many a young lady to wish he belonged to her but he had no eyes other than for his wife, the former Miss Caroline Bingley.

"I am well, Lord Nathan, thank you."

As attractive as Lord Nathan was, he didn't make her heart race. No, that pesky organ only galloped along like a new colt around the vicar's brother, Maxwell Kerr, the fifth Duke of Adborough. Try as she might, no amount of internal scolding changed how she felt around him.

They hit another bump and her maid straightened her straw bonnet.

"Only one more mile, Anna," Georgiana said with a smile.

She returned her gaze to the passing scenery. The rolling grounds of Pemberley's estate. In a few short weeks all this would become a memory. If all went as planned, she'd make her debut, meet a suitable gentleman, fall in love and get married.

Her stomach clenched again.

I have nothing to be afraid of. No one knows about my mistake.

How she longed to capture the carefree girl she'd been before that fateful summer four years ago. Elizabeth, her sister-by-love, cautioned her to move on and forgive herself as she'd been only fifteen at the time, but no one seemed to understand that she'd been more than prepared to become a wife and mother regardless of her age. They all believed her to be a silly girl who'd become caught up in the moment. He'd been a familiar face in a sea of new ones and his ultimate betrayal of her affection cut deep.

She bit back a small sigh and raised her chin, thankful she no longer held a tendré for *him*. That notion had been ruthlessly squashed when she overheard a conversation between him and her brother immediately following their discovery. He informed Fitzwilliam, in a condescending manner, that he'd pursued her solely for monetary gain as no man wanted such a dull flower for a wife. The utter contempt in his tone made her cringe and hang her head in shame.

"You seem rather melancholy, Miss Darcy." Lord Nathan broke into her thoughts. "Are you sure you are up to visiting the Sprague family today?"

"I am well, truly." She smiled to reassure him. "I have been contemplating Pemberley and how much I shall miss it."

"Ah." The quiet assessment in Lord Nathan's eyes told her he doubted the veracity of her statement but wisely kept his counsel. "I see we have arrived."

The carriage slowed to a stop in front of a small cottage. Lazy smoke drifted from the chimney and pretty rosebushes lined the walk leading to the front door, which opened as soon as they alighted from the carriage.

"Miss Darcy, Mr. Kerr. What an unexpected surprise." A rosy faced woman hurried from the cottage and gave them each a small curtsy.

"I brought a few things from Pemberley. Mrs. Reynolds heard how Johnny was feeling poorly and she knows how much he likes peach preserves. There is also some venison and a few cakes."

"Oh, bless her heart, he most certainly does love her preserves." Mrs. Sprague hurried forward and took the basket from Anna, then turned toward the cottage. "Where are my manners? Come in and I'll make tea."

The cottage, though small, was as neat as a pin. Mrs. Sprague took pride in her home and the time spent in her company passed quickly. The physician had been to see Johnny and although still was weak from the fever's lingering effect, he'd rallied enough to sit by the fire and enjoy his tea with them all. About to take their leave, Mrs. Sprague pressed a small token into Georgiana's hand.

"My Henry carved this when he heard you were going to London." Georgiana looked down at the exquisite cross. "We'll keep you in our prayers, Miss Darcy, that God will guide your steps to a good man worthy of your regard."

"Thank you, Mrs. Sprague." Unbidden tears sprang into her eyes. "I shall treasure this, always."

"You just remember to seek the Lord with all your heart and He will guide your path. That verse has kept me and Henry all these years and I like to think the Almighty knows what He's about."

"That He does, Mrs. Sprague," Lord Nathan said. "Your prayers are always much appreciated. Good day." He tipped his hat in respect and Mrs. Sprague gave them both a polite curtsy.

"Good day, Mrs. Sprague." Georgiana joined Lord Nathan at the carriage. After handing her up, he climbed in and sat across from her and Anna.

"That was a thoughtful gift."

"Oh, yes." She opened her hand and studied the cross again. "Mr. Sprague is a talented carver."

The carriage started off with a jolt and Anna squeaked in surprise. The sound was so unexpected, Georgiana began to giggle. The more she tried to stop, the harder she laughed. Soon Lord Nathan smiled broadly and chuckled. Anna, her face red with embarrassment, apologized profusely for having cried out.

"Oh, Anna, you sounded like a little field mouse." She wiped tears of laughter from the corner of her eyes. "I have not laughed that hard in such a long time."

"I'm glad to be of service, Miss Darcy."

Her prim response set off more peals of laughter from Georgiana and this time, even Anna joined in. All Lord Nathan did was shake his head.

"I am sorry, Lord Nathan. You must think us extremely silly."

"Not at all," he gallantly replied. "It has been a long time since I heard you laugh, Miss Darcy. This past year has been good for you. Having Elizabeth's sister keep you company this past winter brought out the fun-loving girl I and my brother's all remember from our youth."

"True, Mary was surprisingly lively and we both shared a love of music. I recall when we first met, she rarely smiled. How I wish she would come to London with me for my debut."

"You know she is not one for fancy parties and large crowds."

"I do know that, but she offers a most sardonic narration of the guests and what makes the commentary so funny is that she does not mean to be satirical. She is only giving an honest opinion and it is so refreshing." Georgiana leaned forward. "She told me during one of our morning visits in London," she choked back a giggle, "that Lady Fitzherbert's hat looked like a peacock had nested upon her head. I had to leave the room before I laughed out loud, but it was true!"

"Poor Lady Fitzherbert." Lord Nathan smiled in remembrance. "I am afraid her milliner informed her peacock feathers were all the rage and, well, she became quite enthusiastic about the whole ensemble."

"Fortunately, everybody loves Lady Fitzherbert. This fashion faux pas will be overlooked because she gives so much of herself to those who need help." The carriage slowed to a stop and Lord Nathan alighted. He turned and gave both women a polite nod. "Tell your brother I shall be over in a few days to discuss the new vicar for Kympton."

"I will. Give my regards to Caroline."

"I shall. She misses your company."

For three months, during Fitz and Lizzy's wedding trip, Caroline resided at Pemberley. Lord Nathan, her betrothed at the time, became a frequent visitor and Georgiana had watched their love deepen and grow. She hoped – no, she prayed – to find a love like that.

At one time she thought his brother the Duke might make an offer. He'd shown an uncommon interest in her each time he visited Pemberley. And, at Lord Nathan and Caroline's pre-wedding ball they'd danced and it was as though she'd come home. The music was secondary to the feel of his strong arm around her waist, his lean fingers holding her hand. Even though she'd worn silk gloves, her skin burned as though he'd physically touched her with fire.

After the dizzying euphoria of the dance he'd bowed politely and returned her to her brother's side. The next morning, she discovered he'd left for London and she hadn't seen him since.

She'd held onto a tenuous hope of him visiting again, but as weeks turned into months the harsh reality of his disinterest set in. She had no choice but to make a concerted effort to seek a husband from another quarter. And for that very reason, her curtsy and debut loomed before her like an executioner's block. She did not do well with strangers. Her thoughts and tongue didn't stay in harmony when she became nervous. It was as though she played Mozart with her left hand and Beethoven with her right. Discordant and confusing.

Aunt Lucinda, the Countess of Matlock, would have an apoplectic fit if she knew where her niece's thoughts were headed. She anticipated Georgiana making a brilliant marriage, as did the whole Matlock/Darcy family. The invisible bonds of duty and family honor continued to spiral around Georgiana's future and at times she felt as though they choked the very life out of her.

Her attention was drawn to the graveled drive leading up to Kympton Parish courtyard. A horse and ride thundered down the lane and pulled to stop beside their carriage. He dismounted in haste and approached Lord Nathan.

"Sir, I am looking for Lord Nathan Kerr."

"I am Lord Nathan Kerr." Nathan met the man who handed him a sealed letter. "Thank you. See my housekeeper for payment."

"Not required, my lord. All of the posts were pre-paid."

"All of them? How many do you have for delivery?"

"Three in total. One for you, one for a Mr. Bingley, and I need to attend Pemberley to deliver one to Mr. Fitzwilliam Darcy."

"I can take the letter for Mr. Darcy," Georgiana interjected, having listened to their conversation. "I am Miss Darcy of Pemberley and am on my way home."

The rider handed her a sealed envelope and she heard Lord Nathan say when he glanced down, "Why, it's from George."

~~~~~~

Georgiana held the sealed letter in her hand and wondered

what news Lord George Kerr needed to impart to both his brother and hers that required incurring the expense of an express post. Dare she hope he'd convinced Catherine to embark on a courtship?

A soft smile formed at the thought of George and Kitty married. One had to be blind not to see how besotted he'd been with her the week leading up to Lord Nathan and Caroline Bingley's wedding. She was fully sure in her estimation that Kitty returned his affection, but Georgiana had witnessed moments when her dear friend, and sister-by-marriage had been most despondent. She fervently hoped the missive contained good news.

She alighted from the carriage as soon as it pulled to a stop in front of Pemberley house and hurried inside.

"Is my brother here?" she asked Carson, handing her pelisse, gloves and bonnet to Anna, who followed her inside.

"I believe Mr. Darcy is in the study."

"Thank you, Carson. I won't need you until later this evening, Anna."

"Very good, Miss Darcy." Anna bobbed a curtsy and hurried up the stairs.

Georgiana tidied her hair as she walked toward the study. The door was not fully closed, so she almost entered without knocking. A soft laugh, followed by the low rumbling of her brother's voice, made her pause.

They're at it again.

She couldn't censure them. Everyone knew how much Fitz loved Lizzy and how much Lizzy loved him. They cared not that Society looked in askance at their open affection. She thought it absolutely heavenly and tiptoed back down the hall a few paces, before turning to face the study door. This time she made her tread a trifle louder than normal and cleared her throat for good measure. She was rewarded by the sound of quick whispers and a swishing of silk.

She knocked on the study door.

"Enter," came the reply.

With a happy smile on her face, she entered the room. She noted Fitz seated at his desk, ledgers spread before him, although one was upside down and his cravat was loosely tied. His valet would be most displeased to see that his handiwork had been tampered with. She then had to bite the inside of her cheek to keep from grinning outright when she also noted his vest buttons did not line up.

Although she'd dearly love to tease her normally staid brother, she gave no evidence of seeing all this as she approached and handed him the letter.

"As I departed Kympton parish, after visiting some of the tenants, a rider delivered an Express Post to Lord Nathan. When he asked for direction to Pemberley, I offered to bring the letter myself."

Fitz accepted the letter from her outstretched hand and turning it over, said, "It's from Lord George."

"Lord George!" Lizzy exclaimed from the other side of the room. "Is Kitty all right?"

Georgiana turned to face Lizzy, who looked far more composed that her brother, although her lips were swollen and her cheeks decidedly flushed.

"Lizzy," she exclaimed, pretending she hadn't known her sister was in the room, "I didn't see you there. How rude you must think me."

"No matter, Georgie. I was reading by the fire and you had no reason to know I was here."

Both she and Lizzy waited as Fitz broke the seal and read the express. His mouth turned up at the corners in a happy smile and his eyes twinkled when he finally glanced up.

"They are to be married," he announced.

"Who? Lord George and Kitty?" Elizabeth asked.

"Yes." Fitz glanced at the letter. "George wrote: *'I shall have to frame the Special License I'd purchased for posterity as my Catherine insists we wait the requisite three weeks, giving her time to arrange a small trousseau and have her sisters from far flung Derbyshire attend the wedding.'* He follows with a date for the wedding and details of Kitty and Mary's travel plans to Town."

~~~~~

"Excuse me, Your Grace," Hobson stood in the door frame to Maxwell Kerr's study. He glanced up from his ledgers and indicated for the butler to enter. "This came by express post. As it bears Lord George's seal, I thought you may wish to attend to it immediately.

"Thank you, Hobson."

Hobson carefully placed the letter on the corner of Max's desk and with a dignified bow, exited the study.

Though intrigued by what George's news might be, Max finished the letter to his steward. One of his tenants had become increasingly difficult, almost to the point where Max considered embarking on a trip to Yorkshire to deal with him personally. However, Mr. Mason was a very competent steward and he'd given him the latitude to deal with it as he saw fit, hoping they wouldn't be forced to evict a tenant whose family had been with the Kerr family for generations.

At times like this, so far removed from Adborough Hall, he felt like he was losing control of his dukedom. There was no way to get around the fact he was required to be in the House of Lords, especially now with all the unrest in northern England. Important bills must be passed to ease the tensions, and that required him to remain in London and exert his considerable pressure on those who waffled in their votes.

The letter completed, sanded and sealed; Max turned his attention to George's missive. He read the first few lines, then leaned back in his chair, letter in hand, and smiled. George had proposed to Miss Catherine Bennet of Longbourn and she'd accepted. Max continued reading and chuckled when George revealed that although he had a Special License, Catherine managed to convince him to wait for the banns to be read.

Good for Catherine, he thought. She had a will of steel, evidenced at Nathan's wedding last year when it was revealed that Viscount Stanhope had threatened her and she had protected George. Max wasn't sure of all the complete details, but George admitted he'd been a spy for the Crown for over five years and because of Catherine's bravery, many lives of British agents in France had been safeguarded.

How shocked everyone had been to discover Stanhope had been a traitor to England, and also, how fortuitous that the Honorable Colonel Fitzwilliam was in attendance to speak with the magistrate and keep the whole affair low key until after the wedding.

Fortunately for him, Nathan's wedding held far more pleasant recollections than vile stories of Viscount Stanhope and his treachery. His best memory, the one he brought to mind on an almost a daily basis, was his too brief of a dance with Miss Georgiana Darcy. Although not formally out in society, she'd been allowed to partake in a few sets at Nathan's wedding ball because it had been held at Pemberley. For a half hour they'd been able to converse without people leaning in to hear what they had to say. Or more specifically, what he had to say.

Their set had concluded far too soon for his liking and he'd returned her safely to a watchful brother. This year she would make her curtsy and he planned to court her. Not in a brash manner like most of the young bucks carried away not only by a pretty face but a handsome dowry. She was far too refined for a direct approach. No, he planned to woo her gently and like a lustrous pearl, coax her out of the shell of shyness. He'd waited a long time for this. A few months would not matter.

Chapter Two

Before the week was out, the Darcy's had arrived in London and were almost immediately beset upon by Lady Matlock and Colonel Fitzwilliam.

"Aunt Lucinda, Richard, you are here at an ungodly hour. We have only begun to break our fast." Fitz stood and gave their aunt a kiss on the cheek.

Georgiana and Lizzy started to push away from the table to stand, but Lady Matlock waved them down. Richard called out a cheery 'good morning' and promptly attended the sideboard. Lady Matlock settled beside Georgiana and accepted a cup of tea from one of the footmen.

"To what do we owe the honor of your company so early, Aunt?" Fitz asked once he'd resumed his place at the table. "Richard, I know, came only to stuff his face with my food."

He gave his cousin a mild glare as Richard sat down next to Lizzy after filling his plate to near overflowing. Richard's reply was to raise an eyebrow and take a bite of his fresh baked roll.

"We have no time to waste," Aunt Lucinda began. "Elizabeth and Georgiana's presentations are but a scant eight weeks away. Not near enough time to accomplish everything I'd like. I have arranged several fittings at Etienne's, for which I am eternally grateful to the Duchess of Adborough. Normally, Madame Etienne has a line weaving down the street for her services, but Margaret was able to exert her influence and hire her exclusively to attend all our girls."

"Caroline and Kitty, as well?" Lizzy asked.

"Oh, yes. Margaret adores both of them and is determined to have them shine this upcoming Season." Lady Matlock let out a satisfied sigh. "There are rumors the Prince Regent himself may attend in honor of Lord George's loyalty to the Crown. I would not be surprised if he doesn't bestow on George his own dukedom."

Georgiana's memory briefly touched on the near-scandal a few days before Nathan and Caroline's wedding. Guests at Pemberley had been informed that a gun accidently discharged in the stables and Viscount Stanhope had been tragically killed. She knew that to be a falsehood as she'd overheard Fitzwilliam and Cousin Richard discussing Stanhope's treachery.

"I hear the Barwick Duchy is vacant." Richard volunteered the information around a mouthful of ham. "At least two hundred acres of valuable farmland and long-term tenants."

"Yes, of course. And there are the secondary titles of Marquis of Glanworth and Viscount Mandeville." Lady Matlock enthused.

"You are a veritable walking and talking volume of Debrett's, dear aunt," Fitz teased.

"You laugh now, Fitzwilliam, but when you and your

lovely bride begin to move among London's finest, you will be glad to know whom to avoid and whom to curry favor with," she decreed with an elegant sniff. "If not for your sake, then for Georgiana's. We expect her to make a splendid match this season. Already there are rumors the Marquis of Trevayne is on the hunt this year."

"Dear God, Mama. You make it sound like he's about to call the hounds." Richard exclaimed. "Trevayne needs to find a wife, that's a certainty, but he is not about to stalk the halls of Almack's and pounce on innocent debutantes their first night out."

"Be that as it may, I expect the foyer of Darcy house to be filled with flowers and cards when eligible gentlemen discover how beautiful my niece is." Aunt Lucinda patted Georgiana's hand.

Georgiana's insides shriveled at her aunt's sentiments. Her aunt meant well, however, she knew, just knew, many eyes would be on her because she was a Darcy and because she was wealthy. Not for the first time she was grateful Elizabeth, Caroline and Catherine would be by her side the whole season.

"Mama would be in raptures if Kitty became a titled lady in her own right," Lizzy said with a laugh. "She will be hard put to remain humble if that happens."

"As soon as you are finished with breaking your fast, we shall meet the Duchess at Etienne's. With six of us to outfit, she will need all hands-on deck."

"Mother, where have you learned Navy terms?" Richard slathered more creamy butter on yet another roll. "Your second and most favored son is an army colonel" – Lady Matlock raised an elegant eyebrow – "one would assume you would use terminology more suited for land warfare."

Lady Matlock waved a hand in Richard's direction, as though shooing his concerns away from her thoughts. "I do know a few Admirals and Navy Captains, Richard. My social circle is quite wide, which you would know if you attended some functions with me."

"Ah, but then you'd expect me to dance attendance on some fresh-faced chit of a girl and make polite talk with dewy eyed innocents."

"Richard!"

"Sorry, Mother. That was quite unchivalrous," Richard apologized, casting a slight eyeroll in the direction of his cousin, Fitz.

They all knew very well that Richard gave no thought, what-so-ever, to finding a wife. He was happily situated as an army Colonel and had no intentions of settling down. Aunt Lucinda would be better served finding a wife for her eldest son, Viscount Ashton. Although, he'd proven just as wily as Richard when it came to avoiding young misses and their ambitious mama's.

"Is Kitty meeting us at the modiste?" Lizzy interjected, obviously trying to move the conversation past the dangerous territory of Lady Matlock's marital plans for her two unwed sons.

"No, George is escorting both Catherine and your sister Mary here. In fact, I'm surprised they've not arrived yet."

"How lovely," Georgiana enthused. "I cannot wait to see them both again. I delight in their companionship very much."

As if on cue, Hutchins appeared at the door for the second time that morning.

"Lord George Kerr, Miss Bennet and Miss Catherine Bennet have arrived. They are in the blue drawing room."

"Thank you, Hutchins. Would you please find out if they would like some tea while we finish in here?" Lizzy instructed.

"Already taken care of, ma'am."

Hutchins gave a polite half bow and left the room.

"Brother, I have finished my breakfast, do you mind if I go on ahead and visit with Mary?"

"Of course, Georgie. We shall be along shortly, that is unless Richard fills his plate again, then it's anybody's guess when we will be free."

"Richard can sit here all by himself. I wish to see my sisters." Lizzy placed her napkin on her empty plate and stood. "Aunt Lucinda, do you care to join us?"

"You read my mind, Elizabeth. I'm more than ready to reacquaint myself with your two sisters."

The three ladies made their way to the drawing room. With one sweeping glance Georgiana noted Lord George next to a radiant Kitty, and, on the couch across from them sat Mary, quiet as always. Georgiana hurried to her side.

"Mary, I am so glad you've come." She took one of Mary's hands in hers as she sat next to her and leaned in to whisper. "Were you surprised by Kitty and George's news?"

"No, even though Kitty swore she'd never marry." Mary replied, her tone exceedingly dry. "As an unofficial chaperone, I witnessed a few encounters between them. The outcome was inevitable, in my opinion."

"It sounds so romantic," Georgiana sighed out. In her mind's eye she pictured Lord George thundering down the lane on a white horse, snatching Kitty up and demanding she marry him. Much like Lord Godfrey did with Lady Desdemona in the latest novel she'd read.

What would it be like to have someone declare their love so passionately? Her breath hitched at the thought of Maxwell Kerr holding her in such a daring way. Maybe even closer than he had during their dance. Close enough for a kiss. Her chest and neck began to flush at the thought. Fortunately, Mary interrupted her wayward thoughts before she turned bright red all the way to her hair line.

"I guess it was romantic." Mary shrugged. "If you believe in that sort of thing." She peered at Georgiana. "Are you all right? You look quite flushed."

"Have you no romantic fantasies? Nothing you've thought about since you were a little girl?" she asked, hoping to divert Mary's attention from her flustered behavior.

"Me?" Mary gave an indelicate little snort. "I have been 'out' in Meryton society for many years with no offers, no interest shown in me by any man young or old, and do not think this will change in the near future."

"The men of Hertfordshire are fools if they cannot see what is set before them." Georgiana declared. About to extol Mary's best qualities, her attention was diverted by her brother and Richard entering the room. Fitz immediately went to George and Kitty, extending his congratulations while her cousin joined her and Mary on the couch.

"You look well, Miss Bennet." Richard said before sitting in the chair across from them.

Georgiana felt Mary start at Richard's words. There was obviously some truth in what she said about men not noticing her.

"Thank you, Colonel."

"Are you still at Longbourn?"

"I remain at home, if that is what you ask." Mary replied through stiff lips and pulled herself more erect than Georgiana thought possible.

"I meant no offense, Miss Bennet. I do not keep abreast of all the gossip and only meant to inquire to your wellbeing."

"I am quite content. In all things."

Well said, Mary.

"Georgiana, are you and Mary ready to leave or does my son require a few minutes to gather more gossip from Hertfordshire?" Aunt Matlock had risen to her feet and looked pointedly at Richard.

"Mother, I am but inquiring after the health of Lizzie's sister and was about to ask if Miss Bennet had continued with her shooting lessons."

A few weeks after the incident with Viscount Stanhope, Richard insisted that Elizabeth and Georgiana know a little about pistols and how to take care of themselves if caught alone and unaware.

"I'd forgotten that you'd instructed the girls in the arts of self-defense." Lady Matlock gave a nervous laugh. "And to think Lady Catherine was concerned about the arts and allurements of young ladies. She'd succumb to apoplexy if she knew you'd shown them how to shoot."

"After the incident at Pemberley, Darcy and I felt it imperative they know how to take care of things if we were not around." Richard turned his attention back to Mary. "Have you continued with your lessons?"

"No, Papa is uncomfortable with me having such a deadly

weapon."

"Such a shame. You had natural talent."

Of the three girls, Mary excelled and had shown an uncanny ability to hit the target at various distances causing Richard to declare that if Napoleon didn't surrender, he would escort Mary to Paris himself and let her deal with the little man.

Often, Georgiana privately wondered if anything would ever blossom from their quirky friendship, but Mary had returned to Longbourn and Richard to his flirtatious ways. As far as she could tell, there didn't seem to be a spark of interest in her cousin's mien.

For the next week and a half Georgiana was busy with fittings and a mad social whirl of afternoon teas, musicales and plays. By the end of the second week she could barely hold her head up and began to nod off at supper.

"Fitz, I don't want to seem ungrateful to Aunt Lucinda, she's done so much, but Georgiana and I are exhausted." Lizzy cast a sympathetic glance toward her. "We are not used to Town hours and I refuse to go out this evening. Do you think Lady Fosscroft would mind so much if we missed her poetry reading?"

Georgiana roused herself enough to murmur, "I truly don't mind—" and hid a huge yawn behind her hand. She smiled, feeling a bit sheepish. "I am tired, but I also do not want to disappoint our aunt."

"Let us continue this discussion in the family sitting room." Fitz signaled the footman to begin clearing the table. "I will send our regrets to Aunt Lucinda."

"Thank you, brother," Georgiana impulsively took one of

his hands in hers and pressed it to her cheek. "You always know how to make me feel more comfortable." To Lizzy she said, "Shall we put on our dressing gowns and have a nice cup of hot chocolate before retiring?"

"That sounds divine, Georgie. It will make us feel like we are back at Pemberley."

"I shall meet you in the sitting room in a half hour."

Three weeks later

Max was seated in a very comfortable chair at White's, a snifter of brandy in his hand. Across from him, sprawled out in his usual, careless way was his newly married brother George and next to him sat Nathan.

"I have to say, after the last month or two, this is a much-deserved respite." Nathan said.

Max silently agreed. The past month had been hectic, what with George and Catherine's wedding and the mad rush to prepare all the ladies for their curtsy before the Queen. Truth be told, he hadn't seen his mother so animated in years. He felt a twinge of guilt. As eldest, he should have maintained some form of entertaining, but that would have opened up a completely different kettle of worms in the form of advanced matchmaking by the matriarch of the family.

"Speak for yourself, brother." George grumbled. "I had to leave my new wife of two weeks to come here and she is much better company than you two clods."

"How is Catherine faring since the wedding?" Max asked.

"She fares very well." The smile that lit up his brother's face told him more than words ever could. "She is nervous about her upcoming curtsy, but having Caroline, Elizabeth and

Miss Darcy alongside eases her disquiet."

"Given what the two of you have been through, a curtsy before Her Majesty will be nothing more arduous than a walk in the park."

"I know my Catherine can do anything, but she's still a young woman finding her way in Society. At times it can be overwhelming."

"Mother adores her and no one would ever cut her direct." Max said. "Their bond was solidified when Mother and Mr. Bennet sat down and shared memories of Father."

"The Lord has a wonderful way of bringing people together," Nathan mused. "If Darcy hadn't gone to Hertfordshire in support of a friend, he'd never have met Lizzy, then I would never have met Caroline and George would never have met Catherine. This was all pre-ordained by God."

"I will add a hearty amen to that," George said. "His ways are not ours and I am much appreciative of His ways." George turned his attention to Max. "What of you, Max? Is this the year you choose a wife? Mother said there are some lovely girls making their debut this year and as a young Duke with a fine estate, you will have your pick."

"I am not rushing to the alter. I wish to marry someone I can respect and love."

"I thought at one time you would offer for Lady Celeste. You were quite inseparable and then – poof – she no longer came around."

"She departed for relatives in Scotland, I believe." He fought the urge to squirm in his chair. Memories of Lady Celeste Townsend were not pleasant ones.

"She married a successful attorney, if I remember

correctly," Nathan mused. "I guess she got tired of waiting for you to propose."

"I never intended to propose to Lady Celeste. She was an amiable companion and that was all."

"Don't get your cravat all twisted over this. Everyone knew she'd set her cap at you," George teased.

Max refused to comment and keep the conversation going. No one but their deceased father knew the perfidy of Lady Celeste. During a house party hosted by his parents at Adborough Hall, Lady Celeste and her parents were one of the many guests. Max had joined his father in the library to discuss estate business. Something they often did before retiring, even if there were guests on the premise.

During one of these sessions, his father had gone to the second level to retrieve an old journal that showed ancient crop rotations. Not the most delightful subject for a young man of one and twenty, but even at that young age, Max knew these were things he should learn. His father had barely ascended the spiral staircase when the door to the library eased open. Upon spotting Maxwell, who had risen to his feet, Lady Celeste entered the room and closed the door behind her.

"I hoped to find you in here."

He felt a slight shiver of alarm, but shrugged it off. He and the beautiful debutante had enjoyed a few dances and conversations and he'd been most impressed by not only her beautiful looks, but charming demeanor. He given some serious thought about approaching her father in order to court her properly and was going to discuss this same matter with *his* father that evening. About to say he would escort her back to the drawing room, and her mother, Lady Celeste moved toward him.

She advanced until their bodies almost touched. "I know you are enamored with me, seeking only the proper incentive to make your feelings known."

Shocked by her brazen attitude, cold fury settled into his heart. He'd been played the fool.

"I assure you, I haven't."

"Not even once?"

Her eyes went wide, disbelief evident. Trailing a finger down his chest, she leaned closer. Max, seeking to evade, took a step back and his legs hit the chair. With a squeal of delight, she launched herself into his arms, propelling them both into the overstuffed chair. It was at that exact moment the door flew open and her mother rushed into the room.

"What do you think you're doing with my daughter," Lady Townsend demanded.

"I believe she's attempting to compromise my son, which you well knew as you were most likely bent at the door peeking through the keyhole."

With a gasp, Lady Townsend's gaze flew to the second floor where his father glared at them over the railing.

"I did not peek through any keyhole. I heard my daughter cry out."

"I'm sure that was your pre-arranged signal to come into the room and find them *dishabille*."

The Duke descended the staircase while Lady Celeste scrambled to her feet and Max moved to the far side of the room.

"What are you going to do about this?" Lady Townsend sputtered in anger as her daughter burst into tears.

"What am *I* going to do?"

"Yes."

"I, Madam, am going to direct my butler to remove you and your family from the premises. The hour is late, you had better attend your packing."

He turned his back to her and moved toward the fireplace.

"You cannot. They must marry!" Lady Townsend took a step toward him, her lips tight with anger or fear, Max couldn't be sure.

"I can and they won't." His father turned around. "You and your daughter set to entrap my son and are no longer welcome in my home. Leave now before I make her shame public knowledge."

"I call your bluff, your Grace," Lady Townsend almost crowed with pleasure. "If you made this public, they would *have* to marry."

"Madam. If this became public knowledge, your family would become social pariahs. I will hold back no facts in the re-telling of the whole story as I saw and heard *everything*."

Max recalled Lady Townsend angrily badgering her father after Lady Celeste ran from the room. All to no avail. His father gave her no quarter and the Townsend's left that very night.

He'd often wondered why Celeste had attempted such a desperate venture until his father quietly advised him, some months later, she'd been seen in Scotland, heavily enceinte with child. That was when he realized how deep her treachery ran and how close she'd come to ruining his chance at happiness.

"I thought his membership was rescinded," Nathan's comment pulled Max out of his reverie.

"Who?" Max twisted in his seat to glance around the room.

With a nod in the direction of the entrance, Nathan murmured, "Sir Reginald Slade."

Slade picked his way through the crowd and joined two other men, known for their outlandish bets and gaming.

"The Marquis of Dorchester brought his membership up to scratch – he said he felt sorry for his circumstances." George murmured quietly. "If Slade would quit the gaming hells, his circumstances wouldn't be so dire."

"I'm surprised Dorchester would do that, considering the old boy had been sniffing around the skirts of his betrothed, Lady Susan for the past six months." Nathan settled back into his chair and sipped his drink.

"Anyone with eyes in in their head knew Lady Susan's only interest lay in Lord Dorchester. Slade's losing his touch if he thought he stood even a ghost of a chance."

Max nodded politely as the Duke of Argyll and his ever-present shadow, Lord Alvanley passed by on their way to the gaming rooms. Immediately Slade rose to his feet and followed them.

"That's not all Slade's lost," George said. "I have it on good authority his estate is mortgaged to the rafters and all his holdings are nothing but vowels in the hands of those he's wagered against and lost."

"How do you find these things out?" Max leaned back in his chair and assessed his brother. Like a dog with a bone, nothing remained hidden when George decided to ferret out truth. "You amaze me."

"I may be out of the game, but I still know most of the

players."

"I for one am glad you are out of the game. It was by far too dangerous."

Max nodded his head in agreement at Nathan's words. George had played a very dangerous game indeed. For over five years he worked for the Crown as a spy, letting any and all believe he was a lecherous cad interested only in the next skirt he could lift. He'd played the part well, so much so even he and Nathan believed the worst of him, convinced his soul was on a perilous ride to an eternity in Hades. They'd had no clue he ruthlessly ferreted out those who would harm the King and Country, making numerous trips to Paris in disguise.

"Slade has made inquiries about Miss Darcy."

"Miss Darcy!" Max almost choked on his brandy and a slight panic chased through his body.

"What type of inquiries, George?"

Thank heavens Nathan had the sense to ask.

"Her dowry and inheritance."

"I must warn Darcy of Slade's intentions." Max murmured.

"I'd offer to carry the message, but as you know I have a young wife waiting at our new house in Mayfair. I should not even be here with you tonight."

"I'll have a word with him." Max placed his snifter on the table and levelled a dark look at George. "Speaking of your new house in Mayfair, remind me to punish you for stealing my under butler."

"Fields? I did not steal him, he volunteered."

Nathan laughed outright and Max gave him a frustrated glare. Their youngest brother shrugged his shoulders and continued to grin.

"Poppycock." Max continued. "Fields has been at Kerr house for almost fifteen years and with Benson nearing retirement, his promotion to butler was imminent. What incentive did you offer?"

"Nothing. I find all I have to do is introduce my beautiful wife and her grace and charm has everyone eating out of her hand within the hour. They adore her."

"Who are 'they'?" Nathan asked and given the tone Max knew he was greatly amused.

"Well... Max might have to hire a new upstairs maid and a few footmen."

"George!"

"Would it help if I told you Fields promised to find another capable man to fill his shoes?"

"Good butlers are extremely hard to come by. You owe me, little brother." Max signaled the major domo to call for his carriage. "Give my newest sister a hug and say hello to all of my previous staff members who have joined you in your new home."

"I shall, and I promise not to pilfer any more staff, although you do have a wonderful cook, and my Catherine loves her strawberry tarts..."

"No. Reconnoiter Nathan's estate and leave mine alone."

"I am not worried," Nathan said with a laugh. "My staff are safely ensconced in Derbyshire, far from Catherine's charms."

"Your carriage is ready, your Grace." The major domo bowed slightly and Max stood.

Even though it was not in fashion, they gave each other a brotherly hug. Max retrieved his cape and hat before proceeding out into the night, his carriage and driver waiting patiently.

"Where to, your Grace?" The driver asked.

"Home, Michael."

Max entered the carriage, closed the door and pondered on the news George had relayed. It bothered him that Sir Reginald Slade was actively gathering information on Georgiana Darcy. This could only mean one thing. When she made her debut, Slade intended to pursue her diligently. He must advise Darcy of Slade's financial troubles. Once Darcy had all the facts, he'd move heaven and earth to protect his sister.

Max knew that between Darcy and his cousin, Colonel Fitzwilliam she was not in any direct danger, however, he'd also maintain a quiet vigilance at social functions. He caught himself smiling. Watching out for Miss Darcy was not a new thing. In fact, quietly observing the beautiful, talented young woman had become second nature. A fact few people were aware.

Chapter Three

"Adborough, this is a surprise." Darcy stood and welcomed Max into his study.

"I wish it was for only a pleasant interlude, but I have come with information which needs to be dealt with quietly."

A light frown marred Darcy's face as he gestured for Max to take a seat near the fire.

"Would you like tea or does this conversation require a more bracing drink?"

"We'll need brandy for this."

Darcy walked over to the table which held the port brandy and cut-glass tumblers. He'd just poured them each a glass when the door to the study opened, revealing Colonel Fitzwilliam.

"I am always amazed, Cousin, how you manage to appear whenever I'm pouring my best brandy." Darcy pulled another glass up from the bottom tray.

"It is a skill which I have honed these many years." Colonel Fitzwilliam advanced further in the room, a cocky grin on his face. "Adborough. 'tis good to see you again."

"You as well, Colonel." Max accepted the drink from Darcy. "How goes the war? Any news from the front?"

"News comes in spits and spots," the Colonel said as he lowered himself into one of the wingback chairs. "We're still waiting to hear the full outcome of Wellington's battle at Toulouse. If it was as a successful as we believe, this could be the end of the Peninsular war, for which I shall be bloody grateful."

"Here, here," Darcy said, raising his glass. "To the end of the war."

"To the end of the war."

They all toasted and quiet settled around them, each lost in their own thoughts. Finally, the Colonel roused himself.

"Did I interrupt something important, or was this the night to get rip roaring drunk and tell bawdy stories all night long?"

"We didn't get a chance to start our conversation." Darcy set his drink down and glanced at Max. "Adborough arrived only a few minutes ago. You, however, only came to drink my port brandy. I am of the mind you hold no affection for me or my wife but covet only my wine cellar," he teased.

"It is much more than that, Darcy. I also covet your cook."

"At least your cousin has not absconded with members of your staff to set up his own house." Max quipped with a laugh.

"Do tell. This sounds much more fun than my war stories."

"It seems George pilfered a few members of my staff. He claims they are falling for the charms of his wife."

"Never doubt the charms of a Miss Bennet," Darcy

murmured. "My household has fallen under Elizabeth's spell and care not for any of my suggestions or worries. Everything revolves around 'what the missus said', or wants."

"I don't think you mind too much, Darce," the Colonel said. "If that self-satisfied smile on your face is anything to go by."

"No, I am happily situated and have no reason to complain." Darcy settled back in his chair. "There is not one thing I can think of that would mar my happiness."

Yes, there is one thing.

Max hated that news of Slade would break into their reminiscing and quiet idyll and was glad the Colonel was here. He'd prove himself a great asset after the untimely death of Viscount Stanhope at Pemberley.

"That brings me to the purpose of my visit." Max set down his drink and braced his hands on his thighs. "George heard rumors of Sir Reginald Slade making inquiries about Miss Darcy."

"Georgiana?" Both Darcy and the Colonel spoke at the same time.

"Yes, Georgiana. Unless you and Elizabeth have birthed a daughter without telling anyone," Max teased Darcy, a grin creasing his face.

"Right. Of course, Georgiana." Darcy placed his drink onto the side table and leaned forward. "What type of enquiries?"

"Of her dowry and value of any inheritance."

"He must know she gets none of Pemberley, not with Elizabeth giving Darcy a healthy son." the Colonel bit out. He stood and began to pace.

"This by itself is not earth shattering, Richard. Adborough must have good reason to bring it to our attention."

"I do. Slade is in over his head. George laid it all out most succinctly when he told me, '*his estate is mortgaged to the rafters and all his holdings are nothing but vowels in the hands of those he has wagered against and lost.*' You'd do well to direct your sister to avoid him at all costs."

"Can we trust what George discovered?"

"George is not given to idle gossip, especially when it's about friends and family. If he has concerns about Slade's intentions, I would not brush them off lightly."

"Is there nobody who can love Georgiana for who she is and not for money?" The Colonel flopped back into his chair. "How many fortune hunters need we fight off?"

Darcy cut a sharp glance at his cousin and Richard abruptly quit speaking, although Max was quite sure he still fumed silently. Max finished his drink and stood.

"I must be off, Darcy, Colonel. Mother has opened Kerr House to receive visitors and demanded I make an appearance and lend support to Caroline and Catherine against would be vipers."

"Should I enlist your aid for Elizabeth and Georgiana?" Darcy asked as he rang for a footman.

"I defy anyone to slander your wife and sister. Your aunt would have them for breakfast and spit out the bones. You forget, I've seen Lady Matlock at work."

"If required, the mater can be quite ferocious," the Colonel drawled from his comfortable spot in the wingback chair. "This is why our mothers are such great friends."

"I'll see you out, Adborough." Darcy stood and opened

the door to the study and addressed the footman who waited. "Please get the Duke's things and bring them to the front entryway."

The footman nodded and hastened away.

"You don't need to see me to the door, Darcy. I've been here enough times to know my way out."

"Nonsense. I'm expecting Elizabeth and Georgiana back any moment and want to see if they've returned."

"Love sick fool!" the Colonel teased.

"One day you will meet a lady who throws you for sixes, cousin, and I for one can't wait to see you fall."

"You'll be a grandfather before that happens."

"Mayhap she will be at the ball your mother is holding after the presentation at court." Max teased. He knew Darcy's cousin flirted with many a pretty girl but rarely singled out any for marked attention.

"Don't remind me of the ball. I plan on hiding in the card room. By the by, Mother is thrilled you and the Duchess are attending," Colonel Fitzwilliam called out as Max and Darcy left the room. "The only dance I shall dance with will be the first one with Georgiana, as promised and then Lizzy. None others…"

With a grin and a nod, Darcy indicated for Max to leave the study, the mutterings from his cousin fading with each step.

"I wish I hadn't been the bearer of such news−" Max began.

"I am exceedingly glad you did apprise us of his debt. Without this knowledge, I might have thought Slade was a good candidate, being that he is knighted with a substantial estate on par with Rosings." They walked side by side down the wide hall leading to the front of the house. "I can't thank you enough, Adborough."

"I think of Miss Darcy as a younger sister," he lied smoothly. If Darcy knew where his thoughts strayed when no one was around, he'd ban him not only from their house in Mayfair, but Pemberley as well. "I wouldn't want any harm to befall her."

"She is a lucky girl to have so many look out for her best interests."

They'd reached the front vestibule just as Hutchins opened the door, admitting Elizabeth and Georgiana. Max's mouth went dry at the sight before him. Clad in a fur lined pelisse and matching bonnet, her cheeks rosy from being outside, Miss Darcy held his attention. She entered the house arm in arm with her sister-in-law, eyes bright with merriment. Everything in him wanted to scoop her up and kiss her soundly. He smiled at the thought. Wouldn't that surprise them all?

~~~~~

"Fitzwilliam, have you come to greet us at the door?" Lizzy cried out upon seeing her husband.

Georgiana came to a complete stop when she spied the Duke of Adborough standing to one side, a footman handing him his cape and hat. Her heart did a traitorous leap at the sight of him, flawlessly tailored in buckskins and high-gloss top boots. His jacket did nothing to mask his broad shoulders, but rather accentuated them. However, it was the rogue lock of hair which flopped down across his forehead that melted her insides. Something his valet would see in horror and immediately apply pomade to curb. Such a shame.

When he returned her gaze, she realized she'd been staring. Immediately, she fussed with her gloves to hide her embarrassment.

"Your Grace, surely you are not leaving as soon as we have arrived," Lizzy addressed Max. "Unless you have dire, emergent business, I implore you to stay for a cup of tea."

"It shall be my pleasure, Mrs. Darcy." Max handed his cape and hat back to the footman with a wry smile. "Although Mother is expecting me at Kerr House to make an appearance for Caroline and Catherine."

Within minutes of their arrival the front entryway was filled with lady's maids divesting them of their coats, bonnets and gloves. Lizzy quietly asked her maid to advise cook to send up tea and cake to the drawing room and Georgiana couldn't help but admire how she'd grown into the role as lady of the house.

"We shall not keep you long and I cannot guarantee you any of the cake or biscuits as we ladies are famished," Lizzy teased as they made their way to the drawing room and their tea arrived a few short minutes after them.

"Are we destitute yet, wife?" her brother asked Lizzy before he sat beside her.

"Not quite my darling, but I am doing my very best to make a dent in that considerable allowance you insist on giving me." Lizzy poured the teas and handed them around. "Fortunately, I still have that lovely dress from last year and it's not too outdated. Madame Etienne need only make a few minor adjustments to the gown."

"Saved from the poor house by my economical wife!" Fitz exclaimed. "Find such as woman as this, Adborough. One who cares not one jot if you have land and money."

Lizzy ducked her head and smiled and Georgiana wondered... what kind of adjustments was Madame Etienne making? She cast her mind back and recalled Lizzy had only dry toast and weak tea this morning, and she'd been sneaking in small naps in the afternoon...

"Have you been enjoying your time in Town, Miss Darcy?"

Georgiana gave a start when Max addressed her directly. She'd grown used to his aloofness, assured he had no time for her and her crippling shyness. She grew more flustered when he settled into the chair next to her.

"I am." She clasped her hands together to stop their trembling "Although I still prefer the company of friends and family more than meeting new people."

"I understand completely. If it weren't for my presence being required in the House of Lords and Parliament, I might never venture into the city."

Caught off guard by his admission, she said, "I thought you enjoyed Town with all its diversions and entertainments."

"You are not the first person to think that, Miss Darcy. No, like you, my ideal of a perfect evening is exactly what we are doing right now. My fondest hope is to find someone who enjoys a quiet lifestyle as well."

And how lucky that girl would be. It was time she began to prepare her heart and mind for when she'd see him courting a more eligible young lady to be his Duchess. Someone with inherent poise and confidence, unlike her.

"Your Grace," Lizzy interjected. "Will you be attending the musicale the Smithson's are hosting?"

"Yes, Mother managed to wrangle all her sons into

attending."

"I've been told the Italian sensation, Senora Angelica Catalini, will perform. Such a coup, as Mrs. Billington has retired and Senora Catalini will be in England for a short time." Georgiana shared the news she'd heard only that morning from their Aunt Lucinda.

"I went to school with the Smithson's son, Cedric." Fitz mused out loud. "Do you remember him, Adborough?"

"I do, indeed. Very studious. Completely absorbed with the study of bugs, if I recall correctly." Max gave a short laugh. "We were forever finding various species of insects in our quarters. He was quite inept at keeping them in their containers."

"Oh dear, I do hope there won't be any crawly things at the musicale." Lizzy fake shuddered. "I'd hate if a beetle chose to climb Senora Catalini's gown in the middle of a complicated aria."

"We shall all be quite safe. I have it on good authority he's been granted a fellowship with the Royal Society and keeps his specimens in a room dedicated solely for his use." Max said and stood. "As much as I enjoy your company, I do have another engagement. Mrs. Darcy, Miss Darcy." He gave them both a polite nod of his head and waited for Fitz to see him to the door.

Georgiana wanted to believe he held her gaze a little longer than the others, but then again, she grasped at any attention he bestowed upon her. If only she were more forthright, more at ease when talking, she might be able to give him a hint of the place he held in her heart.

"Until the musicale, Your Grace," Lizzy said and watched the men leave. "What a charming man. I hope and pray when you find someone, dearest Georgiana, he will be much like the Duke of Adborough."

"Mmmm...." Georgiana did not reply in full, and as she took a sip of her fragrant tea, she couldn't help the one thought running through her mind.

I want that someone to *be* the Duke of Adborough.

Chapter Four

St. James's Palace

"I am immensely proud of you, Georgiana," Aunt Lucinda practically bubbled as she, Lord Matlock and Georgiana waited for their equipage outside the Royal Palace. The line of carriages was long and Elizabeth and Darcy's had departed a few minutes prior. "You have no idea."

"I was so nervous, Aunt. My greatest fear was tripping on my train as I backed out of the room."

"If you were nervous, you didn't show it, dearest."

"Our ride is here," Lord Matlock said as a large carriage bearing the Matlock crest rolled to a stop. Liveried footmen jumped down, opened the door and brought down the stair. Lord Matlock handed them up into the carriage before joining them. Georgiana settled into her seat, careful to arrange her voluminous skirts around her legs so as not to get caught up in the door.

Lady Matlock continued talking about the presentation

and mentioned several times how proud she was of Elizabeth and Georgiana.

"At one time, I wasn't sure about Fitzwilliam's decision to marry Elizabeth. However, she has proven herself to be an able wife and partner and he is so happy with her. She has exceeded everything we could have wished for him."

"So true," Georgiana agreed. "She is my sister-by-love and I cannot imagine our life without her in it."

The carriage rolled to a stop in front of Darcy House and Georgiana exited the vehicle.

"Get a few hours rest this afternoon, Georgiana," Aunt Matlock called after her through the open door. "Be prepared for a long evening of dancing."

"I will, Aunt," she assured her.

"Did I tell you how proud I am of you?"

"My dear, she won't get any sleep if you don't let her enter the house," Uncle Matlock teased.

"Of course, of course. I shall see you around eight-thirty. I want you and Elizabeth to come early so we can make sure your gowns have no tears or unseemly creases before the guests arrive."

Georgiana hurried back to the carriage, leaned in and kissed her Aunt's cheek.

"I love you, Aunt." She gave her uncle a watery smile. "And you as well, Uncle."

"Go on with you," the normally staid Lord Matlock replied, his voice gruff. "You'll never get any rest at this rate."

By this time, Hutchins had opened the door, so she made her final goodbye and entered the house. Fitz and Lizzy had already retired to their chambers, so she made her way up to her room and allowed Anna to remove the feathers and pins from her hair before plaiting it.

She didn't think she'd be able to fall asleep, but almost as soon as her head hit the pillow, Georgiana was gone into the land of Morpheus where she danced all night with a tall, handsome Duke.

~~~~~

"Where could he be?"

Lady Matlock glanced toward the entrance of the drawing room where family had gathered before guests began arriving. Georgiana and Elizabeth had passed inspection, with only one minor delay over a bit of trim on the hem of Lizzy's dress. Satisfied everything was in order, they'd descended to the drawing room to have some drinks and a few finger sandwiches. As the hour progressed, her aunt's state of nerves continued to spiral.

"He realizes how important this is, yes?" she asked for the third or fourth time.

"My dear, he would not miss this unless something vitally significant delayed him," Uncle Matlock soothed.

"Vitally significant? More significant than this ball in honor of all our girls?"

Georgiana had to smile in spite of her nerves. She adored how her aunt included Catherine and Caroline as one of 'her' girls. In the weeks leading up to their presentation they'd spent a lot of time with the Duchess of Adborough and her daughters-in-law. As far as Lucinda Fitzwilliam was concerned, they all were part of the family and she'd defend each of them as one of her own.

Hutchins appeared in the doorway.

"Her Grace, The Duchess of Adborough, Lord and Lady George Kerr, and Lord and Lady Nathan Kerr."

"Thank goodness for reinforcements," Lizzy whispered to Georgiana.

"Indeed, although I am worried about where Richard is as well."

"He'd be here if he could, you know that Georgie."

"Margaret, you look stunning." Aunt Lucinda surged forward and took the Duchess's hands in hers, guiding her to a chair beside where she'd been sitting.

Georgiana looked beyond them, expecting Hutchins to announce Maxwell, but their staid butler closed the double doors and she was left to wonder at the absence of not only Richard, but of Max.

All too soon guests began to arrive and for the next hour Georgiana dutifully stood beside her relatives and received them. When her cheeks ached from smiling and her feet throbbed from standing, the last guest passed by and she could finally follow her Aunt and Uncle to the grand ballroom.

She took it all in with one sweeping glance. From the light of hundreds of beeswax candles sparkling off the chandeliers, to the colorful gowns of Society's finest, the scene was a myriad of swirling colors and smells and for the first time she felt a twinge of happiness edge out the nerves. That was until Aunt Matlock muttered, "Where is he?"

All four of them were in the spotlight of the first dance, a waltz at Fitz's request, and with no partner she'd be forced to stand and watch. The orchestra, hidden from view in a second-floor balcony, began to play the opening bars. A polite reminder for dancers to make their way to the center of the floor.

She twisted her fingers together. If all else failed, Uncle Matlock might dance with her, but he absolutely detested the waltz and there were no guarantees he wouldn't tread on her toes. And her other cousin, Viscount Ashton hadn't descended from the family quarters, so she couldn't petition him for a dance either.

Fitz and Elizabeth, George and Catherine alongside Nathan and Caroline gracefully promenaded onto the dance floor. She knew they were going as slow as possible without being too obvious, and she loved them for it.

She turned to catch Uncle's eye. Trodden on toes were better than not dancing at all, especially if the ball was in your honor. Then she saw him and her breath caught in the back of her throat. Clad all in black, Max stood near the entrance where most of the guests had congregated. Her eyes widened as he confidently strode through the crowd toward her. The cut of his coat seemed to stretch across impossibly broad shoulders and the only spot of color on him was a periwinkle vest which, impossible to imagine, matched the hundreds of tiny embroidered blue flowers trailing down the sheer overskirt which skimmed the floor around her feet.

Max reached her side, took her gloved hand in his and bowed over it.

"Would you do me the honor of your first dance, Miss Darcy?"

Unable to speak, she nodded and allowed him to lead her onto the dance floor.

~~~~~

The following day Georgiana waited in the drawing room of Darcy House with her aunt and Elizabeth, awaiting the inevitable parade of callers. They had to be home for callers, Aunt Lucinda insisted. How else would Georgiana make an excellent match from highly eligible bachelors if she weren't available?

"Last night was an unqualified success, if I may be so bold to say," Aunt said over her second cup of tea, a sure sign of post ball nerves. She never had more than one cup in the morning and would only drink lemon water for the rest of the day. "Did you not enjoy yourself, Georgiana?"

"Yes, Aunt, I did," she answered truthfully.

"I cannot begin to thank the Duke of Adborough enough for stepping in to partner you for the first dance. I realize he's a close friend of the family, but what a coup Georgiana. You are set for the rest of the season. If you don't marry an Earl or higher, I will eat my favorite hat."

Georgiana canvassed her feelings about the ball, and although happy to have received the attentions of various gentlemen, there were none who stood out in her regard. None save Maxwell. She sighed. Would she forever measure all other gentlemen against him? She sighed again. Most likely.

At first, she'd had been terrified of looking like a fool. Thankfully Max arrived in time to partner her for the first dance and then claimed the previously arranged supper set. The rest of the night became a blur of colors and music. Something she'd never dreamed could happen to such a dull flower as she. Her mind tripped back to what she'd overheard between him and Fitz. She hadn't been a dull flower last night. Far from it, if her tired toes could be believed along with all the steady delivery of bouquets this morning.

Stuffed vases filled every crevice of the vestibule and drawing room. The scent alone was overpowering and she'd directed the staff to make potpourri sachets later in the day, but the flowers which she adored and which took precedence over all others, stood alone on the small table by her chair. A simple posy of daisies. Nestled in the fresh cut flowers was a hand-written note which simply stated, 'Congratulations on a successful debut. M.K.'

She was certain he'd pay a call today, if for no other reason than as a friend of the family and when Hutchins opened the door to the drawing room hope flared, only to crash at the announcement of: "Sir Reginald Slade."

"Sir Reginald," Aunt Lucinda greeted him as he approached and gave a very proper bow.

"Lady Matlock." He turned and faced Georgiana and Elizabeth. "Mrs. Darcy, Miss Darcy."

He promptly moved to the chair closest to Georgiana, an engaging smile on his face.

"Miss Darcy, may I be so bold as to compliment you on your attire today? The yellow of your gown makes you shine brighter than the sun."

"I... I... thank you." Georgian searched for words. No one had ever been so forthcoming with praise about her clothing and she wasn't quite sure how to handle such effusive compliments. She sent a silent appeal to Lizzy, who listened intently.

"Sir Reginald," Lizzy solicited his attention. "I'm told you have a lovely estate in Northumberland. Does your family reside close by or do you only see them when in Town?"

"My mother resides with me in Northumberland. She did not attend Town this year for health reasons."

"And you have other family?"

"I have two sisters and one younger brother. My sisters are not out yet, so they are with Mother in Northumberland."

The door opened and Hutchins announced: "The Marquis of Trevayne."

Georgiana caught the sly wink Aunt Matlock gave her and barely stopped herself from giggling. Her aunt was enjoying this far more than she. The butler stood to one side and the Marquis entered, a dashing figure in a finely cut jacket with fitted breeches tucked into high boots. Although quite handsome, he had a decidedly dangerous air about him and also, didn't come up to scratch against Maxwell.

Internally, she chastised herself. She'd done it again. Comparing every man to the Duke of Adborough. Drumming up a quiet smile, she accepted the Marquis' polite greeting, who stopped by her aunt's chair.

"Lady Matlock, it is such a pleasure to see you again. The last time was at the Smithson's musicale and I know you enjoyed that evening."

"I did. Senora Catalini is a marvelous singer. My only regret is we have never seen her perform in a complete opera."

"Then let us hope she returns soon." He turned his attention to Georgiana and Lizzy, his glance sliding over Sir Reginald. "I see I must arrive earlier if I am to garner the best seat in the house." With a cheerful grin, the Marquis settled in the chair across from her and Lizzy.

In the next half hour, three more titled gentleman callers arrived and were dispersed around the room, vying for

Georgiana's attention. Her neck began to tire with all the swiveling left and right, trying to hold several conversations. Finally, after a polite amount of time passed, the gentlemen began to filter out of the room leaving only Sir Reginald Slade who'd not given up his prime position next to her seat.

He was a pleasant enough sort of fellow but she sensed an air of desperation about him. In some ways he behaved in a similar manner to *him*. A little too obliging. A little too subservient. Just a little too much of everything saccharine.

She caught Aunt Lucinda glancing at the clock and wondered '*how did one politely ask a guest to leave?*' Fortunately, her dilemma was solved when Hutchins announced, "His Grace, the Duke of Adborough."

He'd come.

~~~~~

Earlier that morning, before his valet Clarkson had a chance to draw his curtains, Maxwell had lain awake in bed, mulling over last night's activities. He deliberately arrived late for the ball, wishing to lose himself in the crowd, however, before he had a chance to set foot beyond the front vestibule his mother had waylaid him.

"Thank goodness, you have arrived at last," she declared.

Not given to histrionics, he wondered what had his mother in such an uproar.

"I told you I would attend after having dinner at the club. What has you so upset?"

"Now is not the time to dither, come with me."

His mother spun on her heel and walked toward the staircase which led to the second floor and the ballroom.

"Mother, what has happened?"

She paused at the foot of the stairs.

"The Colonel is not here and he is Georgiana's partner for the first dance, which is about to start at any moment. Viscount Ashton has yet to come down from the family area and Lucinda is not even sure if he is in the house. You know how unreliable he can be at times."

Yes, he did know how unreliable Ash could be. He'd known for years.

"What do you want me to do? Ride out and chase down the Fitzwilliam brothers?"

"Don't be daft, Maxwell," Mother scolded. "I want you to partner with Georgiana for the first dance."

And he had.

She'd looked so lovely, standing somewhat alone in her white dress, her gauzy overskirt showcasing a cascade of tiny blue flowers that spilled from her waist down to the floor. He wondered if she noticed his vest. The choice of that shade of blue had been purposeful. In his own, quiet way, he wished to stamp on Society's mind that Miss Georgiana Darcy was his and his alone.

"Shall I draw you a bath, Your Grace," Clarkson asked as he drew back the curtains and allowed the bright sun to lighten the room.

"No, a quick wash and a shave will do."

"Very well, Your Grace."

Clarkson entered the dressing room and Max heard him setting up for his morning ablutions. His first instinct was to rush to Darcy House, which would be foolhardy as Mrs. Elizabeth Darcy's visiting hours were from two in the afternoon until no later than four. He knew, as a family friend he could extend his visit past the stated hours and intended to use this to his best advantage.

Within the hour he was in his study, pretending to read the reports sent by Mr. Mason. He also pretended he didn't hear every quarter hour chime on the grandfather clock in the hallway. Closer to eleven, he made his way to the breakfast room where Mother, Caroline, Catherine and George had gathered to have a light repast before guests arrived at two o'clock. There would be no young bucks attending Kerr House as both Caroline and Catherine were married, but there would be many society matrons and their highly eligible daughters wanting a closer connection to the Dowager Duchess and her unmarried son, the Duke.

For his new sisters-in law he would put up with the lingering looks and unsubtle hints of how 'accomplished' Miss So-and-So was, or how 'well-connected' Lady 'So-and-So was. He had neither the time nor inclination to pander to their lofty hopes and desires. Miss Darcy was a perfect combination of beauty, charm and virtue. His course was set and nothing would deter him.

"Good day, Mother. You look ravishing, as always." He leaned in to kiss the proffered cheek.

"You seem to be in a fine mood this morning, Maxwell. Can I assume you enjoyed yourself at the ball last night? You danced an inordinate number of times for you and never with the same lady twice, other than Miss Darcy, which couldn't be helped – poor dear."

He refused to rise to the bait and decided to keep the conversation neutral.

"I did enjoy myself, Mother. The Matlock's and Darcy's are good friends. Their company always make an evening pass much quicker." He acknowledged his two new sisters. "Caroline. Catherine. I commend you both on a successful first foray into Society."

"The battle is not yet won," Caroline mused out loud. "The true test will come when Catherine and I are out and about shopping, or enjoying a tea on Bond Street. Then we shall see who accepts us for who we are and not who we associate with."

He assessed the former Miss Bingley carefully. He'd always liked the feisty red-haired vixen. She balanced Nathan as no other woman had before and she had a common-sense approach to life, which he also admired. And, she was right. Even with the Duchess of Adborough and Countess Matlock firmly in their corner, some members of society would never take them on as bosom friends.

"You may be correct. However, I assure you there will be no cuts directly, not if they wish to maintain their position in Society. Fortunately, you have no need of their good will. Between all our families combined, we have enough people to hold our own balls and dinners and never need invite anyone else."

"I prefer our own company as well, Your Grace," Catherine said.

"I have told you to call me Max when you are in this house," he teased his newest sister-in-law.

"That will be a hard habit to break, Your Gr—," He lifted an eyebrow. "Max."

"Much better." He turned his attention to George. "Have

we heard what happened to the Colonel? As far as I could tell, he never made it to the ball."

"No, he didn't. My sources informed me he was called to Spain." George told them all.

"To Spain!" Mother exclaimed.

"With Napoleon's abdication after the battle at Toulouse, many English assets are on the move and need safe passage home. There have been some pockets of resistance within France, so they are migrating south."

"But why would Colonel Fitzwilliam be dispatched to Spain? Lucinda must be frantic."

"Mother, the Colonel is not a paper soldier but a battle worn veteran. His knowledge of the area and ability to think ahead make him necessary for securing some of our deeply imbedded agents."

"Do we have any idea when he may return?" Max asked.

"No, although with the armistice having been signed a but a few weeks ago, I pray everyone returns safe."

"I pray that as well," Catherine added with much feeling. At Max's questioning look, she added, "A friend is in France and has been there for over a year. His family believe him lost as they hadn't heard from him since he joined the army, but through certain circumstances George and I know he is in France as a spy."

"And you've not told his family this?" Caroline asked, clearly astonished.

"No. First, for security reasons we cannot tell them what he is doing or where he is and second, why raise their hopes of his being alive only to find out later he may not." Catherine took George's hand in hers. "This has been on my heart and mind since your wedding, Caroline and I pray everyday he returns safe. All I can do is trust."

"As you know, my Catherine is a most persistence woman of prayer. I think God will allow her friend to return if only to stop her from banging on the gates of Heaven." George quipped, giving his bride a soft smile.

"George, stop teasing your lovely wife," Mother chided gently. "Every mother wants someone to pray for their son when they are at war. I know I did." She caught and held Catherine's gaze. "You continue on, my dear and I shall add my voice as well."

~~~~~

The clock had chimed three times when Catherine approached Max in the crowded drawing room.

"Your Grace, may I introduce Lady Standish and her daughter, Miss Penelope Standish?"

Max, engaged in conversation with Lady Addlesworth, turned slightly. The first thing he noticed was Catherine's nervousness, shown by the way she squeezed her fingers together. He cut a quick glance across the room and saw George, glowering in the corner at Lady Standish. George would make his life miserable if he didn't do something to allay Catherine's nerves.

"You do not need to stand on formality, Catherine, I have told you to call me Max."

He'd caught the calculated way Lady Standish eyed his new sister and wished her to know Catherine was a treasured member of the family, not someone she could order about, which is what he suspected by this intrusive introduction. He turned fully to face Lady Standish and her daughter, who was passably handsome but not handsome enough to tempt him from his first love, Georgiana.

"Your Grace." Lady Standish had the intelligence to lower her eyes as she sank into a graceful curtsy. Miss Standish also curtsied with a murmured 'Your Grace' but didn't seem too impressed, which amused Maxwell to no end. Mama Standish may wish her daughter to snag a Duke, but the daughter obviously had no intentions and he decided he'd like her on that fact alone. For Catherine's sake, and George's, he suffered Lady Standish and her inane prattle of Penelope's accomplishments until the clock struck the quarter hour.

"We were delighted to meet your new family members. When my daughter Penelope made her curtsy, we both commented on how delighted your Mother seemed."

"Mmmm... yes," was all he said. Undaunted, Lady Standish continued to prattle.

"Penelope immediately asked for an introduction, knowing they would become great friends. I have it some authority—"

"Pardon me, Lady Standish, but I have another appointment and must take my leave."

At that time, with a polite bow to both ladies, he excused himself from their company, not caring one jot if Lady Standish thought him rude. He intended to arrive at Darcy House at precisely three-forty-five and watch all the other hopeful suitors leave while he stayed behind as a 'family friend'.

"Well. I never..." and "Yes, you have, Mama," was all he heard as he moved to his mother' side and in low tones informed her he was leaving.

His carriage awaited him, as per instructions and within minutes he was on his way. After being announced, his heart leaped in his chest at the look of joy Miss Darcy bestowed upon him. He also noted flowers on the table beside her. His flowers. What didn't please him was the sight of Sir Reginald Slade seated next to her. Had Darcy not warned her about him?

Chapter Five

Max barely had a chance to greet everyone before Darcy appeared beside him with a murmured, "Adborough".

"Fitzwilliam. I had not thought you would join us today," Elizabeth said, extending her hand to him when he stopped by her chair. "We've been having a lovely conversation with Sir Reginald. His family did not come to Town this year, so he is a free bird, it seems."

"Indeed," Sir Reginald said, bobbing his head in agreement. "Mother was not well enough to attend this season."

"We don't wish to keep you further, Sir Reginald. Please convey our regards to your Mother when you write her next." Darcy ushered Slade toward the door of the sitting room. "Hutchins will see you out."

Oh... I don't—" Slade stammered.

Hutchins magically appeared and with a small flair of his hand, indicated Sir Reginald to follow him. Clearly befuddled, the man could do nothing else but trail behind the austere butler. It was only when the door closed that Lady Matlock directed her glare toward Darcy.

"I have never seen you hustle someone other than your Aunt Catherine out of your home with such speed. Please explain your behavior."

Max moved across the room and took the chair vacated by Sir Reginald. Georgiana gave him a lovely smile and then turned her attention back to her brother and aunt.

"Do you remember our conversation this morning and I told you there was a gentleman we need to be wary of?" Darcy began.

"Yes… Oh!" Elizabeth started to frown and then understanding dawned. "He was the man you spoke of?"

"Yes, excuse me one moment." Darcy walked to the door and called to the butler, who appeared a few seconds later. "Hutchins, we are not home to Sir Reginald Slade and he is NOT to be granted access for any reason. Please inform the necessary staff."

"As you wish, Mr. Darcy."

"Nephew, what is this all about?"

"I have been given some confidential information about Sir Reginald, and suffice to say he is not a desirable suitor for Georgiana."

"Not desirable? He has an estate that rivals Rosings and has been knighted by the King."

Lady Matlock cast glances at both Darcy and Elizabeth.

"If I may, Darcy," Max interjected.

"Please do."

"My brother George has a way of discovering hidden truths and it came to his attention that Sir Reginald is heavily in debt. Due to some unfortunate decisions on his part, which I will not relay, Sir Reginald needs to find a wife of means." Max heard a soft intake of breath from Georgiana and turned to her. "I am sorry to be so blunt, Miss Darcy. I would never wish to offend your sensibilities, but you need to be aware that some men are not who they seem."

"I'm more aware than you know, Your Grace."

"Georgiana," Elizabeth surged to her feet, casting a cryptic look at her husband, "the day is still young and we have not had our walk today. Would anyone care to join us?"

"I shall pass, my dear." Lady Matlock stood as well. "I have been tardy in my correspondence and it refuses to go away on its own. I will inform my staff to be wary of Sir Reginald as well." She gave both Elizabeth and Georgiana a kiss on the cheek before exiting the room. Elizabeth turned to Darcy with a bright smile.

"And you, dear husband? Are you willing to traipse about the bushes in the park across the street with your sister and me?"

"You know I will." Darcy glanced at Max. "You are welcome to join us, Adborough, but be prepared for more than a sedate stroll. Lizzy is used to rambling the grounds of Pemberley and finds the park too confining. You may find yourself circling the same grove of trees several times."

"I am not that bad, Fitz." Lizzy playfully swatted at his arm. "I'm quite content to walk only the perimeter today."

Max relished the idea of some uninterrupted time with Georgiana, albeit under the watchful eye of her brother. "I believe I shall go with you. The day is yet young and the weather agreeable."

Within fifteen minutes the four of them exited Darcy House and crossed the street to the park, several sturdy footmen following at a respectable distance. Upon Max's quizzical look, Darcy said, "One can never be too careful."

"I concur," Max agreed with a nod. He then paused and waited for Georgiana while Darcy and Elizabeth followed.

"I understand your curtsy and first ball was a success." He glanced down at Georgiana, wishing the brim of her bonnet wasn't so wide. Although she looked lovely no matter what she wore, he wanted to see her face. To gauge her reaction to him.

"As I've never been presented, nor attended a full ball before, I rely on family to tell me whether it was a success, and my aunt is well pleased, so I guess it was."

"I am glad for you. I wish nothing but good things for you, Miss Darcy."

"Th… thank you."

He noted her small stutter and knew from past experience she stumbled in her speech when nervous. To allay her nerves, good or bad, he began a gentle conversation about her time at Pemberley before coming to Town, which led to her telling him about the visit with Mrs. Sprague, one of their tenants.

"Her husband made this for me." She reached into the pocket of her pelisse and brought out a carved cross. "They have so little, yet still took time to give me something before I left."

"May I?" He held out his hand and she placed the cross into his palm. He turned it over and examined it carefully before handing it back. "The fact that your tenants think highly of you is commendable, Miss Darcy. You will be a fine mistress of an estate one day."

And that estate will be mine.

As though she'd heard his thoughts, she raised startled eyes to his and with satisfaction he saw a blush rise on her cheeks. Just as quickly she lowered her gaze and tucked the cross back into her pocket. All too soon their walk ended and Max went home content, knowing he would see Miss Darcy at Lady Dalrymple's ball in a few days' time.

~~~~~~

Georgiana smoothed the front of her dress in an attempt to calm her nerves while she waited for her next dance partner to make an appearance. The whole Darcy/Matlock clan attended Lady Dalrymple's Ball along with what seemed like most of London's beau monde. If success was rated on how crowded, on how uncomfortably hot, or on how loud a room could become, then Lady Dalrymple would be very pleased indeed.

However, it wasn't the press of bodies that had nerves stretched tighter than a violin string, it was the ever-present Sir Reginald who'd sniffed her out like a basset hound almost as soon as she'd entered the house. Now that she was aware of his dire need of an heiress, she had no intention of giving him encouragement of any kind. Fortunately, she'd been able to stay one step ahead of him, but it seemed her luck had finally run out.

Darcy and Lizzy were dancing. Aunt and Uncle Matlock had been waylaid by Lord Patrick Grayson, who had some news of Cousin Richard, and her other cousin, Ash had made a bee line for the card room, bypassing the ball room completely. She was stranded on the edge of the dance floor and noted Sir

Reginald beginning to skirt the edges toward her.

Carefully, she eased back and made to turn. If nothing else she could retire to the lady's room and pretend to fix something on her gown. What she hadn't counted on was Sir Reginald to cut directly across the floor and step into her path.

"Miss Darcy," he simpered with a low bow in front of her.

"Sir Reginald, you surprised me."

"I hope you mean that in a good way, Miss Darcy." He reached for her gloved hand but she flicked open her fan and used it too cool her face. He had no choice but to drop his arm. "I have stopped by your home to pay my respects, but you have been one busy young woman. I did leave my card."

His voice held censure as well as a touch of disappointment.

"I have been busy indeed, Sir Reginald. My aunt has a great many friends and wishes me to make their acquaintance. I'm sure you understand."

Where was her family? She stopped herself from glancing around. It would not do to let Sir Reginald know she was uncomfortable in his presence. It would also not be wise for Sir Reginald to discover that one time, when he'd come by Darcy House, she was home and heard Hutchins outright lie and inform him the family was out. What amazed her even more was that Sir Reginald had the audacity to query their loyal butler as to where she and Lizzy had gone.

"May I have the next dance, Miss Darcy?"

"Thank you, Sir Reginald, but my card is full."

She spoke a partial truth. Between family members, close friends, the Marquis of Trevayne, The Earl of Litchfield and the Earl of Dunleavy she has a surfeit of partners. The only exception being the very next dance and the supper set. She'd deliberately left those blank with the hope Maxwell would request her company for one of them.

"May I see?"

She gasped. A gentleman never demanded to see a lady's card.

"Sir Reginald—"

"Excuse me, Sir Reginald. Miss Darcy promised this next dance to me."

"Your Grace!" A flood of relief washed through her body at the sound of Max's deep voice. She turned and gave him a proper curtsy. Max returned with a slight nod and held out his hand.

"Are you ready, Miss Darcy?"

"Oh yes, thank you." She placed her gloved hand in Max's and moved closer to him. "Good evening, Sir Reginald"

As they strolled to the dance floor, she noticed that the color of Max's vest was the same soft green as the trim of her gown and the ribbon in her hair. What a strange coincidence. First, his blue vest matched her embroidered flowers and now her ribbons. If he weren't careful, people would begin to think they were a couple. Not that she'd mind, but as he'd never given any indication that he thought of her in 'that way' she didn't want any rumors to float around.

"I am sorry that I was late, Miss Darcy," the Duke began.

"No need to apologize, Your Grace. You weren't on my card."

"I meant in the fact I was not there to forestall Sir Reginald imposing himself upon you."

She glanced up and saw a look of anger chase across Max's

handsome face. She couldn't help herself, she blushed and stammered, "Th... thank you. I appreciate your concern for my well-being. You are a dear friend."

"I am more than a friend, Miss Darcy."

The look he gave her caused her stomach to flutter. If she were fanciful, she could almost believe he cared for her. And not as the sister of a good friend, but maybe something more. He led her to the head of the formation and they faced each other as the orchestra began playing the opening bars.

Not once did Maxwell remove his eyes from her face. They came together, touched hands briefly and parted one again, and his gaze never wavered. As they moved down the line, he had to watch his other partners, but did not emit the same intensity he'd given her.

Heat blossomed in her chest and at times she fought to keep a grin from escaping. The other dancers would think her deranged if she let go and laugh out loud. Dare she hope the Duke of Adborough held her in high enough regard to court her? Maybe his choice of vest color was deliberate and not something of chance.

She'd been led astray before by fanciful thoughts. This time she would proceed with caution and wait for him to declare his intentions. Too soon the dance was over and Max escorted her to where Fitz and Lizzie waited. Beside them stood the Marquis of Trevayne, her next dance partner. With a polite bow over her hand, Max left her staring after his broad shoulders as he cleaved through the crowd.

A soft hand at her elbow alerted her to the fact the Marquis was ready to lead her to the dance floor. With a smile, she let him guide her to the starting position. More than once, she caught the Marquis studying her. Rumors were rampant he was on the hunt for a bride and she idly wondered if he had considered courting her.

He was so very attractive and if she weren't in love with Maxwell, her heart would be in danger around the handsome lord. The dance was lively and their conversation flowed as easily as a bubbling river. When the last chords of music faded away, and they'd bowed and curtsied, he led her to the refreshment table.

"May I speak openly with you, Miss Darcy?" Trevayne asked as he handed her a glass of punch.

"Please do."

"I enjoy your company very much, however, I am not looking to take a bride, regardless of what you may have heard."

"Oh, I've not..." she demurred.

"You are not one to lie easily, my dear. Do not start now.

She had the grace to blush.

"I tell you for two reasons. One, I enjoy your company and wish to dance without worrying if the woman expects a proposal the minute the set ends."

"And the second reason?"

"You, my dear, love another man."

Heat blazed across her cheeks and she clenched her jaw to keep her mouth from falling open. Had she been that obvious? Her eyes darted across the dance floor toward Lizzie. Had everyone seen how foolish she was? She needed to leave – now!

"Are you well?"

"No... I mean, yes... I don't..."

"Take my arm."

The Marquis held out his arm and led her towards the terrace. Once outside, he dropped his arm and she wrapped her arms around her midsection, not caring if she wrinkled her dress.

"I'm so…sorry for my discomposure," she whispered and looked out toward the garden. Was her love for Max so obvious? How foolish everyone must think her, especially as he'd given her no cause to hope for a return of feelings.

"Miss Darcy." The Marquis' firm tone captured her attention and she turned her face to him. "I had no intention of ambushing you with this observation. In fact, I'm sure most of society has no idea you hold a certain Duke in such high regard. You are a lady in every sense of the word and have done nothing wrong."

"Then why…? I mean, how…?" Her mind whirled like a child's top and she couldn't, for the life of her, find the words to so many questions she needed answers for.

"How did I see what others have missed?"

"Yes!"

"First, I will admit that when I first met you it did cross my mind that you would make a gracious Marchioness. My mother would find you lovely, my sisters would easily befriend you and my brothers would gnash their teeth in envy at my finding such a suitable woman."

"Oh… Thank you."

"However, because I paid more attention, I noticed you become more animated whenever a certain gentleman approached. Nothing ostentatious, mind you, but your eyes light up and the softest smile graces your beautiful face. When he is near, you are content."

"You are very observant, my Lord."

"It also has not escaped my notice that he is quietly exerting his influence as well."

"In what way, if I may be so bold to ask."

"I think you know. Lately the two of you have been... well-matched?"

She bit back a small gasp. Maybe her intuition that Max had paired his outfit to match hers was not as crazy as she thought. The Marquis offered her his elbow and they moved back into the ballroom, toward Fitz and Lizzy. A few feet from her brother and sister, the Marquis murmured, "There is another who watches you even more closely than I."

"Who would that be?"

"Normally, I wouldn't share the name of a would-be suitor, but I've heard disturbing things about this gentleman and I wish you to remain cautious of him."

"Now I truly must know the gentleman's name, unless it is the Prince Regent. I would never say no to dancing with him."

"You are a delight, Miss Darcy. No, it is not Prinny who has you in his sights, thank the good Lord for that, but it is Sir Reginald Slade. Be on your guard."

They had reached her family and with a gallant bow over her hand, the Marquis said farewell and melted into the crowd.

"Did you enjoy your dance with the Marquis, Georgiana?" Lizzy asked, her eyes bright with amusement. "The two of you were in deep conversation. I'm sure everyone saw how well he regards you."

Georgiana faced Lizzy and smiled. "He is a kind and gentle man. Some lady will be very lucky to be his wife, but that woman will not be me."

"Did he ask to court you, Georgiana?" Fitz asked, his voice deep with concern.

"No, brother, he did not, but that does not mean we did not have a meaningful conversation and I am very sure he and I will be good friends."

"Miss Darcy, I believe this is our dance."

She turned to face the Earl of Litchfield. "My Lord, I believe you are correct."

Chapter Six

Max strode to the outer edges of the dance floor, trying hard not to look anyone in the eye. He had no desire to speak with a soul before he recovered his composure and paced to the end of the hall. He slipped into a small alcove which overlooked the entire ball room and watched as Georgiana took the floor with Trevayne. A sharp pain stabbed through his heart at the sight of her in the arms of a man who was not her family.

He did not regret his dance with Georgiana, even though his name was nowhere on her dance card. Why? Why did he not leave her alone?

Because Slade is a snake in the grass and I cannot stand the thought of him touching her.

He quietly acknowledged he was annoyed by several things, one of them being too many eligible men swanning about Miss Darcy. He tried to find fault with them, but none had any egregious bad marks against their character. Other than the fact they breathe, he silently groused.

The dance ended and instead of escorting her back to her

family, the Marquis accompanied Georgiana to the refreshment table. Was that a blush on her cheeks? What poetic nonsense was Trevayne spouting? Her eyes widened and her mouth fell open and all color fled from her face. Had Trevayne just proposed as she held a glass of lemonade? She looked as though she might cast up her accounts any moment. Trevayne escorted a visibly shaken Georgiana through the terrace doors. Blast and damnation, he couldn't see them through the panes of glass. Dare he intervene? Could he intervene if she had accepted an offer of marriage?

They're not yet at the altar.

He still had hope.

An eternity later the couple came back inside and Max released his breath.

"What has you so entranced, Adborough?"

"What?" Max turned to see Ash standing beside him.

"I've called your name several times, but you were intent on something, or someone in the ball room."

Max fumbled for a response. It wouldn't do to blurt the truth to Miss Darcy's cousin. *I'm sorry I missed your approach. I was debating whether to run Trevayne through with a sword and then carry off your cousin, or to have a glass of wine. Quite the dilemma, don't you agree?*

No, he would error on the side of caution and lie through his teeth.

"Sorry about that. I was debating the merits of Lady Dalrymple's watered-down wine against her equally insipid lemonade."

"Really," came the dry observation, accompanied by an arched eyebrow which told Max that Ash did not believe him for one minute.

"Why are you here, hiding in a darkened corner? I thought for sure you'd remain at the card tables until every young miss of marriageable age had given up hope and gone home."

"I had to leave." Ash gazed out over the ballroom, his lip twisting into a lopsided grin. "If I had to listen to the mindless chatter of Lord Ramsey and Lord Fosscroft about their bad knees and gout for one more minute, my right eyeball would pop out and roll onto the table. Could you imagine the gossip?"

Max couldn't help it, he laughed out loud. A few matronly chaperones along the wall turned and peered intently into the darkened alcove, trying to see who lurked in the shadows. He and Ash simultaneously moved out of their line of sight into the hall.

"More to point, what would your fellow card sharks say?" Max asked.

"His eye popped out, right out onto the table. Made for a dreadful mess, we had to locate a new pack of cards." Ash's grin widened. "Fosscroft, poor sod, wouldn't know what to do. Without his wife nattering in his ear, he'd forget to put one foot in front of the other while walking."

"That's a bit harsh, even from you."

"Forgive me, Adborough. I'm feeling a tad testy. Mother is determined to see me and Richard marry. More to the point, see me marry and bring on the requisite heir." Ash gave Max a considered glance. "How do you deal with your mother? Surely with two of her three boys settled she's anxious for the Dukedom to be secure."

"She's hinted here and there, but for the most part keeps her counsel. I've not had to hide at balls or take my meals at

White's to avoid her, unlike a certain Viscount."

"That will all change." Ash pushed away from the wall he'd leaned against. "The Season has just begun and as the heat rises, so will all the mama's expectations for their daughters. Mark my words, your mother will corner you, and soon."

"I'm surprised there's not a wager on that very thing at White's."

"I've already placed ten pounds on you to marry before Michaelmas."

If things go my way, you'll win that ten pounds.

Max couldn't help but quip, "I can't believe my marital status is of any interest to anyone."

"You have one of the richest Duchies in England. Everyone wants to know who you will marry."

"Everyone?"

"Yes, you conceited puss. Everyone." The Viscount gave him a small farewell salute. "I'll see if I can't start some salacious rumor."

"Uncalled for, Ash," Max grumbled as the Viscount wandered off.

About to return to the ballroom, his mother's voice stopped him.

"There you are."

Max turned to see the Duchess advance toward him.

"Mother, you look lovely as always."

She offered her cheek and he gave her a light kiss.

"I hadn't seen you come into the ball room and had to be told by others that my son was dancing," she gently chastised.

"My apologies. Almost as soon as I arrived, I noticed Miss Darcy being harangued by Sir Reginald. I whisked her onto the dance floor before he could press upon her further."

"George told me briefly about his circumstances and Lucinda filled me in on the rest. You are a good friend to the Darcy family." Max acknowledged her praise with a nod. "Have you decided who you will dance with next?"

"I haven't even had time to greet my host and hostess. Dancing will come later."

"You are not getting any younger, Maxwell, and the only way you will find someone is to actually go up to them and begin a conversation."

He gave a small start at the idea of his mother querying his marital aspirations so soon after his conversation with Ash.

"Mother, I am barely one and thirty, hardly in the grave!"

"Not that I wish to bandy my age about, Maxwell, but I wish to have a grandchild before I reach the age of fifty. You and your brothers have but three years to grant me my wish."

"I am sure my siblings shall accommodate you within the year."

Mother sniffed elegantly. "Only because they have acquired a wife, which you seem reluctant to follow suit."

"I have yet to meet a woman I wish to spend my life with," he said smoothly. "I want the same felicity and joy you and Father had."

"I must point out that our joy began when your father asked me to dance. Maybe you should follow in his light-as-air footsteps and seek to do the same."

"I will do my very best." He leaned in and kissed his mother's cheek again before whispering, "Beyond that I cannot promise more."

"You do that or I shall make a list and find you a wife

myself." His mother took her closed fan and tapped him on the arm. "I am determined to see you well married by the end of this Season."

"I'm leaving now, Mother."

"You are lucky I love you as you are." She smiled at him. "Come and sit with me after the supper set."

"You know I will."

As it was, Max had to leave the ball a few minutes before midnight.

"Harold," he exclaimed upon seeing one of his footmen approaching. "Why are you here, of all places?"

"Pardon me, Your Grace, Mr. Benson sent me with an urgent message for you to return to Kerr House."

"Did he say why?"

"No, Your Grace, but I do know he received an express from Adborough Hall."

"Very well. Tell Benson I shall return immediately." Max didn't hesitate in this decision. Benson was an extremely reliable butler and would have interrupted his evening only for the most extenuating of circumstance. "First, I must find my host and bid her goodnight and then let the Duchess know I am leaving."

"Yes, Your Grace." Harold bowed properly and turned to leave.

Max searched the crowd for Lady Dalrymple and upon sighting her, cleaved his way through the crowd.

"Ah, Your Grace, you are a sight for sore eyes." Lady Dalrymple held out both her hands, which Max took possession of and bowed over them giving a light squeeze before dropping them. He'd known her all his life and loved her like a family member. As always, she blushed slightly at the safe, yet flirtatious move. "You look perplexed, my boy. Are you not enjoying yourself?"

"I am, but sadly I must take my leave."

"So soon? The clock has yet to strike midnight and the night is still young. Many young lady's hearts will break when your handsome face no longer graces my ballroom. I know my cousin Miss Elizabeth Elliot was hoping for an introduction. She and her father, Sir Walter, arrived only this afternoon from Bath."

"Urgent business calls me away. The introduction to Miss Elliot will have to wait for another time." He executed a polite bow. "Thank you for a lovely evening."

"I'll forgive you this time, young Adborough, and only because I adore your mother."

He smiled. "You have excellent taste in friends, Lady Dalrymple. I bid adieu."

The next few minutes were spent checking the various nook and crannies his mother liked to occupy at these types of gatherings, finally locating her in a retiring salon. Quickly, he related all that he knew and requested she pass the information along to their friends. He regretted not saying his own proper good-byes, but Mr. Mason was not one to send word if the situation wasn't calamitous in nature. He donned his cloak and stepped into the inky night, wishing once more he was back in the ballroom with Georgiana on his arm.

~~~~~

Georgiana pulled a brush through her hair and stared at the mirror without seeing her reflection. All her thoughts were consumed with her dance with Max, followed by her dance with the Marquis and subsequent conversation. Sadly, the empty slot on her dance card, the one she'd saved for a handsome Duke had been filled by her cousin, Ash.

The Marquis' observation of how Max's vest matched her dress sent a secret thrill though her body. It hadn't been her imagination. Her heart sped up at the thought and a light blush danced across her cheeks. If the Marquis noticed, had anyone else? And if true, why wouldn't Max declare himself and at least propose a courtship.

She put down the brush and blew out a soft breath. It was so frustrating to be a female, always waiting for the man to take the lead, or make a move. If she were more forward, she would have declared herself three years ago.

Anna, her lady's maid, bustled into the room. She picked up Georgiana's ball gown and gave it a slight shake. "Not too wrinkled, Miss Darcy. Did you have a nice time? You came home so much earlier than I expected."

"I did have a lovely time," Georgiana said with a slight smile, not willing to confide that after Max left the ball all things previously beautiful lost its lustre. When Lizzy mentioned she was feeling tired, Georgiana readily agreed to leave. "I don't think I'll be able to sleep a wink tonight."

"Would you like a nice cup of hot milk?"

"That would be just the thing."

"Right then," Anna draped the ball gown over her shoulder and opened the bedroom door. "I'll put this away first, and then pop on down to the kitchen."

"Thank you, Anna."

Anna closed the door and Georgiana went into the small

sitting room attached to her bed chamber. The fire was low, but the room was comfortable enough she didn't require a robe over her nightgown. She sat in one of the wingback chairs and picked up the letter she'd received from Mary Bennet that afternoon. She'd been so busy getting ready for the ball she'd had no time to read the chatty letter. Anna would be at least a half hour before she returned, so this was as good a time as any to catch up on news from Longbourn.

Lizzy has written that she and Jane are both in Town along with Kitty, and you all had a most successful curtsy before her Majesty. I am so relieved Papa didn't make me join you, even though Mama pouted a bit when I stayed firm in my decision. I have no intention of ever marrying, and even if I did, when would I be in the midst of high society? No. I think I shall be a most favored aunt who spoils her nieces and nephews most atrociously.

Mama seems tired of late. I think all this excitement has finally worn her down. Granted, she's more involved with the tenants now that Lizzy and Jane are no longer here, and she's quite busy in the still room making soaps and candles with Hill. I dearly miss Kitty's lavender sachets. Little did we realize how much each sister contributed to the running of Longbourn. The hallways and rooms of our humble abode seem quite empty these days.

When not busy in the garden, or helping Mama write down our expenditures in her journal, I spend my time reading and have begun learning the new music which you so graciously sent last month. Mozart is my latest favorite composer. I marvel at his talent.

How I miss playing duets with you, dear Georgiana and look forward to this fall when my Aunt and Uncle Gardiner take me with them on their annual pilgrimage to Derbyshire. Even my young cousins shall attend this year. Prepare for epic sea battles with my nephews on

the lake so fortuitously situated near the house and delightfully elegant
tea parties with my nieces. That is, unless you do something outrageous,
like fall in love and marry—

An unfamiliar cracking noise outside had Georgiana lay the letter down. She crossed to the window and drew back the curtain, hoping an animal had not become trapped on the balcony.

Although the moon partially illuminated the yard, she saw nothing, but then there was movement in the tree which loomed over the balcony. About to scream, she caught her breath when a large tabby cat landed on the balcony, spotted her through the glass door and arched its back and hissed.

"You frightened me, mangy old cat," she said with a shaky laugh. "No more bits of chicken and ham if this is how you thank me."

The cat turned its back and padded to the edge of the balcony, nimbly leaped back onto the tree and melted into the darkness. Georgiana dropped the sheer curtain which hung over the door and moved to her bedroom. She slid beneath the covers of her bed and a large yawn stretched through her as she waited for Anna to return.

~~~~~

The letter from Max's steward painted a grim picture. One of his tenants claimed a neighbor killed his prize cow. From there, they'd proceeded to fisticuffs with death threats being bandied about. Max knew both men and for the life of him couldn't understand how things had escalated to such outlandish proportions.

He made the decision to leave immediately and cover as much ground as he could without falling asleep in the saddle. He and his men would take a few hours to rest at one of the many posting inns dotted on London Road and be in Yorkshire by early evening the next day. The ancient grandfather clock struck half hour after one as he and his outriders cantered through the quiet streets of London on their way to Adborough Hall.

~~~~~

The soft light from the inn was a welcome sight. After four hours in the saddle, Max craved a warm bed and good food. He instructed one of his armed outriders to ride ahead and secure a suite of rooms.

"Almost there, Pericles." He soothed his mount and the proud beast tossed back his head in reply. "I'll make certain there are enough oats to fill your belly, my lad."

He urged Pericles forward to meet his returning outrider, James.

"There's plenty of room, Your Grace," his man said. "I didn't tell him who you were; only that you were a gentleman of means needing a room for the night. He also has rooms above the stables for the men."

"Let us get on then."

Within minutes, he and his men dismounted in a warm spacious barn. Even though he was a Duke, he still stripped off Pericles' saddle and brushed him down. His horse cared not one jot that he was a nobleman and Max enjoyed taking care of the ornery beast. Assured there were enough oats for all the horses, he turned to leave the barn.

After confirming their departure time with James, he entered the Waddling Duck, greeted by a portly man with the largest mustache he'd ever seen. Brown eyes that looked like berries twinkled at him.

"We're honored to have you here, sir." He gave Max a small bow. "I'm the owner, Mr. Barrows."

"I do not require much beyond a room for a few hours, unless your cook has anything left over for a small meal for me and my men."

"Aye, she made up a large pot last night. Told her we'd have to throw it all out, she'd made so much." He chuckled as he fetched a room key. "Then my Betsy said – if you're married, you'd know the tone – 'The good Lord told me to make this stew,' and that was the end of the argument. Good thing she did. Another gentleman checked in not five minutes before you arrived, but he took his meal to his room. I know there's more than enough for you and your men."

"Excellent." Max had to smile as the older man chattered. "I will have my meal now, and then attend my room. Would you be so kind as to knock on my door at nine o'clock? I need to be on the road by ten at the latest."

"T'will be my pleasure, sir."

Mr. Barrows hurried off and Max made his way to the private dining room. In a few minutes, a young girl, bearing a remarkable resemblance to the rotund inn keeper entered the room carrying a huge bowl of aromatic stew and a small loaf of bread. She set them down and returned with a mug of ale.

"Will there be anything else, sir?"

"No, this is quite satisfactory."

"Yes, sir." She curtsied and hurried from the room.

After thanking the Lord for his meal and safe journey he dug into the stew, grateful it tasted as good as it smelled. A half hour later, pleasantly sated, he made his way to his room on the second floor and almost groaned at the sight of the bed. He'd been awake for almost twenty-four hours and it was only sheer will-power that drove him to place one foot in front of the other.

He'd removed his cravat and pulled his shirt from his breeches when he heard a woman cry out. The sound came from the room below. He waited a few seconds and hearing nothing more, started to remove his shirt. A scream pierced the air.

Without thought that his shirt was undone and loose about his hips, he strode from the room and in less than a minute stood outside the door to the room below his. Sounds of a struggle, although muffled, filtered through the door.

Disgust arose in his chest. He had no idea who occupied the room, or whether it was the man's wife or a woman from the village in the room with him, but by the sound of it, she wasn't a willing companion. The thought of any man forcing himself upon a woman, married or not, made his stomach turn and with one well-placed kick he booted open the door.

The sight before him was chaotic. All the bedclothes were scattered about the room, as though someone had jumped on the bed, or scrambled across it to evade. A woman cowered on the floor beside the bed and a man clad only in his breeches, his back to the door, held her ankle in his left hand, his right had raised above his head as though to strike. The woman's nightgown, twisted around slender thighs, had risen enough to reveal several bruises and one deep cut on her creamy skin.

"Unhand that woman!" Max bellowed.

The man turned and Max was stunned to see it was none other than Sir Reginald Slade, who whirled around and after a momentary hesitation swung his fist at Max's face. Max feinted to the right, then ducked and tackled Slade around the waist, thankful that years of wrestling with two younger brothers gave him a decided edge.

The momentum of their collision carried them onto the bed, which collapsed beneath their combined weight. A brief struggle ensued, ending when Max managed to punch Sir Reginald solidly on his chin, who fell back onto the mattress, his body limp. Assured Slade would not come around any time soon, Max turned and kneeled beside the woman, her face obscured behind a tangled curtain of dark golden curls.

"You will not be harmed." Hesitantly, he touched her shoulder, not wanting to frighten her further. "Lend me your hand; I will take you to safety."

The woman finally raised her tear stained face and his heart stuttered to a stop.

"Miss Darcy!"

Chapter Seven

A noise from behind snapped Maxwell out of his shock. Mr. Barrows stood within the door frame, his cheerful face now twisted into a mixture of worry and anger. In his beefy hand, he held a club of some sort.

"I don't allow this kind of behavior in my inn——" he growled, lifting the club in a threatening gesture.

"Mr. Barrows, this lady needs care." Max snatched a blanket off the bed and draped it around Georgiana's shoulders. No one else needed to see the state she was in. "Have someone attend the stables and request one of my men to come here to guard Sir Reginald."

"Who are you to give me orders? For all I know, you're in on this with him," Mr. Barrows sputtered in anger.

Max rose to his feet, Georgiana in his arms, and towered over the man.

"I am the Duke of Adborough." Mr. Barrows blanched at the mention of his title. "I have nothing to do with this sordid piece of humanity other than saving the lady from his clutches."

The innkeeper lowered the club and gave him a quick bow.

Max continued. "Would you ask your daughter bring some salve and warm water to my room. This lady requires attention."

"Right away, Your Grace."

Max hurried upstairs, distressed by the small whimpers Georgiana tried to hide by pressing her face into his chest. He immediately placed her in a chair and without thought pulled back the blanket to assess if her wounds were dire. At her gasp, he realized how inappropriate his actions were and quickly threw the blanket back over her legs.

"Forgive me, Miss Darcy. I was so worried about you I wasn't thinking straight."

"N... n... not to worry, Your Grace." She choked back another sob. "I was trying... I was... t...t...t...trying..."

She burst into tears.

Max fell to his knees and society be damned, placed his arms around her slender shoulders and pulled her against his chest. "Hush. You are safe. He cannot hurt you now."

"I know." He felt her head nod in time with her statement. "Th..." She drew in a shuddering breath. "Thank you."

"Can you tell me what happened?"

He felt her head shake in the negative against his chest and heard a stammered whisper. "N.. n... not right now."

"Shh...., you are safe now. Mr. Barrows is sending his daughter with salve to soothe the injury to your leg."

A long shudder rippled through her slim body and Max drew her close to his chest, his mind whirling with the ramifications of what transpired. If the inn keeper was a discretionary soul, he would not spread the gossip further than the four walls of this room. However, Slade was an entirely different ball of wax. His main purpose in this heinous act was to force Miss Darcy into marriage for her substantial dowry, and he alone might engage in slanderous gossip to achieve that goal.

Max looked down at the tangle of curls against his chest. How long had he dreamed of holding Georgiana in this manner? There was no way he'd allow Slade to triumph. He'd planned on courting her in a slow, gentle manner and that course of action had been brutally demolished. As soon as he could get word to Darcy, he'd apply for a Special License and he and Georgiana would marry as quickly as possible.

There'd be some whispers, but over time everything would be forgotten in the wake of yet another society scandal. As the granddaughter of an Earl along with being the Duchess of Adborough, no one would ever cut her direct. He'd make sure of it.

~~~~~

In the midst of showing his wife how much he adored her shapely curves, Darcy cursed at the firm knock on their bedchamber door. However, knowing his valet would not disturb them for anything other than an emergency he quit the bed, donned his robe and opened the door to a visibly upset Hutchins. To see his normally unflappable butler in a state of agitation sent an icy chill along his spine.

"I am sorry to disturb, sir, but Anna has brought distressing news."

Darcy stepped out into the hall, giving Elizabeth time to

set herself to rights.

"What has happened? Where is Anna?"

"She is in Miss Darcy's bedchamber." Hutchins squared his shoulders. "Miss Darcy is missing."

"Missing? As in not her room, or as in not in the house."

"Not in the house, sir."

By now, Lizzy had come out of their bedchamber, tightening the belt of her robe around her waist, luscious curls of hair cascading over one shoulder.

"What is going on, Fitz?"

"Georgiana is missing."

"Oh no!" Lizzy rushed down the hall to Georgiana's room, followed closely by Darcy. Anna stood by the fireplace, her face a picture of worry. Other than the bedclothes strewn about the floor in an untidy heap, nothing was out of place.

Darcy almost ran to the adjoining sitting room and immediately noted the balcony doors were wide open, the curtains swaying in the gentle breeze. A thick rope, tied to the largest pillar, dangled over the rail, pooling into a small puddle on the ground.

He gripped the balustrade and cursed.

"Fitz, come here."

Darcy re-entered Georgiana's bedroom and Lizzy handed him a smaller rope.

"I found this on the floor."

"They must have used this to tie her up and then lowered her over the railing. Like an animal." Whoever did this to his sister would pay and pay dearly.

"Do you think they took her for ransom?"

"That would be an obvious answer, however, the prize

might be her dowry. It all depends on who is desperate enough to go to such lengths." Darcy turned to Hutchins. "Have a footman take a note to Matlock House, and use someone who has great discretion. There is no need for this to go beyond our families."

"Yes, sir." Hutchins gave him a slight bow and disappeared down the hall.

"Anna, did you see anything unusual this evening?"

In his mixture of anger and fright, Darcy had forgotten about Georgiana's lady's maid. Thank the good Lord for Lizzy's clear thinking. He waited alongside his wife for her answer.

"No, Mrs. Darcy. Miss Georgiana said she was too excited to go to sleep right away, so I offered to make a cup of warm milk." She waved her hand toward the desk where an abandoned cup of milk sat cooling. "When I returned, this is how I found the bedchamber." Anna fished a handkerchief out of her pocket and wiped at the tears streaming down her face. "I was only gone for about a half hour."

"It took you a half hour to warm up some milk!" Darcy exploded and took a step toward the maid, his anger getting the best of him. Lizzy's hand on his forearm stopped him. At the sight of Anna's eyes, wide with fear, he drew himself up straight. "My apologies, Anna. I'm beside myself with worry."

"I understand, sir. I had to hang up her ball gown first."

"Anna, you may go to your room and we will speak further in the morning. Please do not speak of this to anyone." Lizzy soothed, tugging Darcy back to her side.

"Not a word will pass my lips, and thank you, Mrs. Darcy." Anna curtsied and hurried from the room.

Lizzy faced Darcy, cupping his face with her palm.

"We will find her, Fitz. Now go, write that note and I'll canvas a few other servants who were awake to see if they noticed anything out of the ordinary."

He turned his face to kiss her palm. "What would I do if I lost you, my Lizzy?"

"That is something you never have to worry about." She placed her hands on his shoulders and gently turned him around to face the door. "Now go."

By the time Darcy had penned a letter and sent a footman to Matlock House, Hutchins attended the study with one of the stable boys.

"Mr. Darcy, Clive is one of our stable boys and he may have some information."

"What do you know, Clive?"

"I saw a large gray carriage on the street. It were there fer a couple of hours."

"Did you see who was in the carriage?"

"No, but I kept a look-see, 'cause the driver were watching the 'ouse."

"That was very astute of you, Clive."

The boy flushed, "Thank you, Mr. Darcy."

"When was the last time you saw the carriage."

"It were a little after you and the missus returned. I'd finished beddin' down the 'orses, when I 'eard a noise. I followed me knack, thinkin' it 'ad sumthin to do wif the carriage and saw a man carryin' a woman. I now know it 'ad to be Miss Darcy. 'E placed 'er in the carriage and took off at a right fast pace."

"Why didn't you tell anyone sooner?"

"Clive came forward before I'd even begun to canvas the

servants, Mr. Darcy." Hutchins interjected. "He didn't know whom he should tell as the stable foreman had the night off."

"Thank you, Hutchins." Darcy once again focused his attention on the stable boy. "Did the carriage have any distinguishing marks?"

"Not that I could tell, 'ceptin' the front wheel. It were a different color. Like it were new, and the 'orses didn't match. The lead set were a nice pair of greys, there were a bay and the other dark, almost black." The boy scratched behind his ear, as if in thought. "Mr. Darcy, sir, I can't say for certain, but the man looked like that bloke what's been comin' around. Sir Reginald or sumthin' like that."

Darcy looked at Elizabeth, who had wrapped her arms around her midsection, her face etched with worry. The both said together, "Gretna Green."

Darcy dismissed the servants and got dressed while his valet packed a small valise. Lizzy, unable to sleep, watched from a chair beside the fireplace.

"How far do you think he'll get before he has to stop for a rest?"

"I don't—"

"Colonel Fitzwilliam is in foyer, sir." Hutchins called through the door.

"Richard!" Darcy hurried out of the room, valise in hand and Lizzy followed.

They found Colonel Fitzwilliam pacing the front entryway, slapping his riding gloves against his thigh with each step.

"Richard, when did you arrive home?"

"Earlier in the day, after everyone had left the house. I

wasn't prepared to attend a ball and so I spent a quiet evening at home. Now, enough of this trivial nonsense, tell me what has happened."

Darcy proceeded to fill Richard in on everything he knew, finishing with, "We have no time to waste. We have reason to believe Slade took her and will head for Gretna Green. He obviously didn't expect us to realize Georgiana was gone until morning, maybe even early afternoon."

"That is to our advantage, but at the same time we're going to have to stop at every inn along the way to make sure she isn't there."

Although Richard spoke in a deadly tone, Darcy sensed the same anguish in his cousin that clutched at his belly and squeezed. He feared what would happen to his sweet sister when Slade had her alone, in a room with no where to go.

"Sir Reginald will want to put as much distance between him and London." Lizzy mused out loud, her tone thoughtful. "All the inns closer to Town have too many people who could recognize them both. No, I believe he'll travel a few hours before stopping."

"She's right, Darce. We have the advantage as we will be on horseback."

"What if you take the wrong route." Lizzy cried out. "What if Sir Reginald takes a less traveled road?"

"Then he runs the risk of wasting too much time and I'll be waiting for him at the border." Darcy said with determination. "No, my love, I believe Slade will take the route that is fast and easy. Don't forget. He thinks he has a ten-hour or more advantage on us."

"I pray you are right, Fitz. I truly do."

Soon, Lizzy bade them farewell as they mounted their horses and set off with grim determination toward Scotland, assuming Slade would make haste to Gretna Green, hoping no one would miss Georgiana until the next day.

They rode hard the first hour and then eased up for the next few so their horses would stay reasonably fresh and began checking the stables of all the inns situated near the main road. Neither of them gave voice to the despair that clutched their hearts.

After being in the saddle for almost three hours, they came upon the Waddling Duck and within the stable was a large gray carriage, with a mismatched wheel. Without saying a word, they handed their horses off to the sleepy stable hand and almost ran to the inn. Upon their entrance, loud voices and the sound of a scuffle filtered down from the second level.

Richard began to scout around the main floor while Darcy impatiently waited for the owner of the inn to appear. About to search the inn without permission from anyone, a portly man, wielding a club, rushed past him and headed toward the kitchen.

"I say, sir..." Darcy called out to no avail. He leaned over the counter and tried to peer into the kitchen, determined to catch the attention of the man when, if, he returned.

"Nothing down here," Richard said as he returned to wait with Darcy. "Where is everyone?"

"That is what I am trying to determine—" The man with the club exited the kitchen area, his face a bright cherry red. Darcy didn't know if it was from anger, ascertained by the death grip he had on the club, or from all the running about he'd been doing. Given the state of his body shape, Darcy was quite sure the man didn't give over to too much exercise other than a good belly laugh.

"We are not accepting guests." The man panted out.

"I do not require a room. I'm searching for a young woman. A lady. Tall, dark-haired—"

The man hefted the club and made like he was about to strike Darcy. "Are you in on this as well? My inn is not a bordello, where women are bought and sold!"

"What!" Richard blurted out. "What are you saying man? We're here to rescue her!"

"Who are you?" The man didn't budge an inch, glaring at each of them in turn. Behind him, a young girl who looked very much like the inn keeper, slid by. She carried a bucket of hot water and an armful of cloths. Darcy's heart plummeted to his feet.

"We are family. Where is she?" Darcy managed to grind out.

The man assessed the Colonel and Darcy. He gave a quick nod, then said, "Follow me."

They trailed him up the narrow stairs, nearly running into his back when he stopped at a room where the door had been kicked in.

"You get your smarmy arse back into that room, or I'll make sure you stay down for a few days," the man snarled.

"I shall call the magistrate!"

Darcy recognized Sir Reginald's voice immediately. He stepped behind the innkeeper and glanced into the room. What he saw sickened him. Slade's face lost all its color when he spied who towered behind the portly man.

"Where is my sister?" The icy tone in Darcy's voice

shocked even himself. He never thought of himself as a violent man, but given time and no witnesses, God Himself only knew what he would do to the man standing amongst strewn bedding.

The innkeeper gave him a surprised look before turning his attention back to Sir Reginald. Slade slid to the floor, next to the bed which was clearly ruined and lowered his head into his hands. The very thought of Slade attacking his sister in such a forceful manner as to break the bed made him want to cast up his accounts. With dread resolve, he determined if that were the case, Slade would not see the light of another day.

"She's on the next floor, second door on the left," the innkeeper said, maintaining his vigil of Slade. "The Duke of Adborough took her to his room. One of his men is supposed to guard this vile blackguard."

"Adborough!"

Richard and Darcy exchanged glances.

"You go, Darce. I'll stay and keep good old Reggie company until reinforcements arrive."

Richard advanced into the room and Sir Reginald scuttled on his backside into a corner and cringed. Without so much as a backward glance at the coward who may have ruined his sister forever, Darcy sped up the stairs and charged into Max's room. In one sweeping glance he saw the young girl from downstairs gently applying salve to a large cut on his beloved sister's leg. Georgiana, a blanket draped about her shoulders, clung to Max, weeping into his shoulder.

Chapter Eight

The return to Darcy house remained a bit of a blur to Georgiana. Richard insisted on lacing her tea with small amounts of laudanum to help ease the pain incurred from the injury her leg along with the bruising on them and her back. For the next few days she stayed either in her rooms, or joined Lizzy in the family's private drawing room on the second floor. Although her memory was murky, before leaving the inn she recalled a conversation between her brother and cousin and knew they were deeply indebted to the innkeeper's daughter for her skillful ministrations.

"Georgie hasn't sustained life altering injuries, Darce." Richard had said. "The wound, though deep, will heal given time. Mr. Barrow's daughter certainly has the hands of a healer. I doubt your physician could do any better. Besides, the fewer who know of this debacle, the better."

"Yes, I know," Fitz had acquiesced. "Would that I could take this from her."

Her poor brother. How many times must he rescue her

from men with nothing but darkness in their hearts? Deep in thought, seated next to Lizzy, Georgiana gazed out the window. Thank goodness for Maxwell. If he hadn't come along when he did… She shuddered.

"Are you well, Georgiana?"

Lizzy's gentle query shook her out of her morose thoughts.

"I was but thinking of His Grace and how thankful I am he was there to… there to…"

Lizzy reached out and covered Georgiana's hand with hers. "He saved you and for that we are eternally grateful." She picked up her piece of embroidery. "Fitz told me the Duke has requested a meeting today."

"Oh…" Georgiana smoothed the blanket covering the lower part of her body with trembling hands. She hadn't spoken with Max since that dreadful night. How much of her body had been revealed in the struggle with Sir Reginald? Almost as soon as Sir Reginald carried her into the room at the inn, he'd dumped her on the bed and ripped her nightgown in an attempt to grab her breast while removing his breeches. In her desperation to evade, she hadn't cared about her state of undress. She'd twisted and squirmed to no avail, and then, remembering something Richard told her after the incident with Wickham, she'd kicked Sir Reginald between the legs. Her only thought had been to stop the attack, never once thinking he'd retaliate with such fury. She remembered each stinging blow and how helpless she'd felt as she kicked against the maniacal grip on her ankle.

Fitz and Richard both assured her Sir Reginald would never bother her again. Although they'd not told her what transpired, she believed strongly Sir Reginald had been given no option other than deportation. She need not live in fear anymore.

She raised her gaze to Lizzy's and smiled. "I do hope the Duke stays for tea."

"Darling Georgiana, if he were able, I believe he would, but you are not receiving visitors until tomorrow. I'm sure we can expect him to stop by again."

"Oh," she whispered, not daring to let her heart hope. "I wish to thank him. For everything."

"Then let us make sure you follow doctor Lizzy's orders so those dressings may come off." Lizzy moved a small footstool closer to Georgiana's legs. "Legs up, my dear. Doctor's orders."

"If I didn't adore you so much, dear sister-by-love, I'd throw my favorite pillow at you." She dutifully lifted her legs and stretched them over the cushioned stool. Lizzy fussed with the blanket and then settled back into her own chair.

"Much better. Would you like me to continue reading Cowper?"

"Yes, please, favorite sister-in-law."

"You minx. I'm your only sister-in-law."

"Then it's a good thing you're my favorite."

Lizzy laughed and leaned closer to lay her hand over Georgiana's.

"I am so glad you were returned to us relatively unscathed. I'd miss your shy smile and teasing. I'm quite in love with you, alongside your brother."

"I am glad too, Lizzy."

The ladies spent the next hour conversing and reading and

Georgiana dreamed of tomorrow.

~~~~~

"His Grace, the Duke of Adborough." Hutchins intoned at the door of Darcy's study.

"Thank you, Hutchins. Have cook send up some tea."

"Very well, Mr. Darcy."

Hutchins backed away and gave Max a polite nod as he entered the study. Darcy was seated at his desk, but upon him entering the room he leaped to his feet and came around the desk.

"Have you just returned from Yorkshire?"

"I did, only this morning." Max advanced into the room. "How is Miss Darcy faring?"

"Much better, thank you for asking. She is moving around although the doctor has forbidden her from leaving the house. The physical wounds are healing—." Darcy stopped when his voice cracked with emotion. "If you hadn't intervened…"

"I thank God daily that I was there and think back with horror of what might have been." Max sat in the chair Darcy offered. "What happened to Slade?"

"My cousin offered him two options." Darcy sat in the chair opposite Max. "Either accept the offer of deportation or take his chances with Richard. Alone."

"Ah… I hazard to guess he is being quietly deported?"

"Yes." For the first time since he'd arrived, Darcy smiled. "Although, Richard did have some quality time with him before your men arrived to guard Sir Reginald."

"Can't say I disagree with your cousin's methods." Max couldn't stop the wince from crossing his face.

"Richard's reputation in the army is well earned. Slade picked the wrong heiress to abscond with."

"He did indeed."

"Enough dredging up of that night, let us look to a bright future where the sun shines continuously and nary a cloud in the sky."

"Darcy, I've never known you to wax poetic. Your wife's influence is beginning to peek through."

"No influence, Adborough. I have always been a romantic, it's just that the ladies of the ton expected so much I dared not show any emotion. A quirk of an eyebrow was almost synonymous to a proposal."

"How true." Max laughed softly. "Mother told me once how Clarissa Featherington was absolutely heartbroken when I did not pay my respects after smiling in her direction at Lady Addlesworth's ball."

"Had you smiled in her direction?"

"I honestly don't know because I did not even know what Miss Featherington looked like. Nathan had to point her out at the next soiree we both attended."

"I suppose you do understand what my experiences were like." Darcy stroked his chin in a thoughtful manner. "I presume that is why I adored Lizzy from the start. She didn't give two farthings what I had by way of land and money. She was far more interested in how I treated people. We had some interesting conversations of my attitude."

"By conversations, I assume you meant arguments?"

"Absolutely. The best one was the first time I proposed to her."

"You proposed more than once?" Max stared at his friend,

shocked at his admission. "That means she refused you?"

"Yes, she did," Darcy said with a secretive smile crossing his face. "And rightly so. I was an absolute prig."

"I find that hard to believe. You are the epitome of politeness and social etiquette."

"There is an inherent problem of looking down from the lofty heights of social standing."

"And what would that be?"

"While I was busy looking at all the faces of those beneath me, all they saw was the hind end of a gentleman."

"Darcy!" Max started to laugh and couldn't stop. He'd never heard the master of Pemberley speak so plainly before. "Where in the world did you come up with that?" he finally managed to choke out.

"In one of our more private arguments, my wife succinctly pointed this out." Darcy grinned. "And, she was right. My Lizzy is always honest with me and I wouldn't have it any other way."

"I believe your marriage has balanced you in ways you're only beginning to understand."

"Now that is a true statement." Darcy settled back in his chair and assessed Max. "This conversation has been pleasant, but I'd like to know the real reason you have come by today. I know you continued on to Adborough Hall after the incident at the inn, but to return in under five days is quite remarkable, even for you."

"Most of the groundwork had been taken care of by my steward. I convened a meeting between the two tenants. Fortunately, we worked things out I was able to leave a few days earlier than expected. I was most anxious to return and find out how Miss Darcy fared."

"As I reported, she is well, all things considered." Darcy still watched him carefully, his next words measured. "And that is the only reason for your visit today?"

Max swallowed hard. The one thing he'd dreamed of was about to come to fruition.

"I've come to request your sister's hand in marriage."

"There's no need, Adborough. Richard offered to step into the breach if…" Darcy stood and ran a hand around the back of his neck. A sure sign he was embarrassed.

"If nothing better comes along?"

"Well… yes." Darcy stopped harassing his cravat and walked a few steps toward the fireplace.

"And you believe you can do better than a Duke?" Max teased with a slight smile. "You do know the next step above me is Royalty?"

"It's not that," Darcy said. "I don't want you to feel obligated because you were the one who rescued her."

Max joined him by the fireplace and stared into the flickering flames. Was it safe to reveal how deep his feelings were? He finally lifted his eyes to Darcy and decided on a more cautious approach.

"I can assure you my intentions are honorable and I hold your sister in the highest regard. Even without this debacle, she is someone I have considered as a wife."

Darcy held his attention with a steady gaze for a few long minutes and Max returned it with calm regard. Finally, he nodded. "I accept your proposal on behalf of Georgiana. I shall contact my solicitors to begin drawing up the marriage settlements."

Relief swept through Max's body at those words, and he

couldn't help but tease his normally stoic friend. "Do you not think I should ask your sister if this is something she wishes?"

"Georgiana has no other option. Marriage is the only way to save her reputation and I cannot think of another man more capable than you to make her happy."

"Even though I'm not her cousin?"

"Especially since you are not her cousin," Darcy said with a grin. "I'll shall send direction straightway to Klemper & Bedway, my solicitors."

Darcy crossed over to his desk and sat down. He pulled out a few sheets of paper, an inkwell and quill. Within minutes he'd had most of the letter written.

"I'd forgotten how exceptionally fast you write." Max said, thinking back to their University days and wondered at the whimsical smile that crossed Darcy's face. "Did I say something funny?"

"Not really, it was more of a remembrance from the time when I first met Elizabeth and we were both at Netherfield Park."

"Ah, I see. Mrs. Darcy appreciated what fine penmanship you have."

"Not at all. It was your sister-in-law, then Caroline Bingley, who expressed her appreciation." Darcy chuckled. "At that time in her life, I could have sneezed and Caroline would have gone into raptures. She is much altered since meeting your brother."

"Yes, and Nathan is very appreciative that she no longer holds you in such high regard."

"I'm almost done. All I need is the direction to your solicitors and we can have things set up before the week is complete."

"Excellent." Max took one of Darcy's sheets of paper and scribbled down the address of his solicitors in Town. He straightened and smoothed out his coat. "Am I able to see your sister today?"

"Normally, I would say yes, but Georgiana has only begun leaving her quarters and as such is not dressed for company." At Max's quizzical look, he expanded. "The dressing comes off tomorrow and then she can wear a gown. I'm sure you understand."

"I will come by in the afternoon, and if she feels up to it, pose my question and let her know she does have an option, regardless of what you may say."

"Adborough, I'd love to give her leeway in this regard, but like it or not, Georgiana must marry and I don't think I could ask for a better brother-in-law."

"The sentiments are returned. I look forward to a long and felicitous marriage."

"After you speak with Georgiana, I shall post the announcement and start the process of reading the banns. This gives you three weeks to make plans and give the appearance of a courtship. With luck, no gossip will seep out, but we must be prepared for anything."

"Are you sure you weren't the one trained in strategy, Darcy. Your cousin would be most proud to hear you talk like this."

"Good or bad, Richard tends to rub off on people. Be careful when you invite him for dinner. He makes you laugh at off color jokes and you will find yourself sipping more brandy than thought possible."

"I shall take that under advisement, although, in his day, my youngest brother raised a few eyebrows. He experienced harrowing times in France that changed him body and soul and I don't believe your cousin could surprise me with any stories that don't rival Nathan's."

"I forget how jaded Nathan was when he first returned. When I think of him, I see the man he became. Lizzy once observed that we are to think of the past as it gives us pleasure."

"Sage advice. We should listen to your erudite wife more often."

"It certainly makes for a happy marriage."

"I can't wait to discover this myself." Max said to his soon-to-be brother and thought, with a smile, in three weeks, Georgiana will be my wife.

Chapter Nine

"His Grace, the Duke of Adborough."

Although prepared for his visit, Georgiana couldn't help the little breath that somehow caught at the back of her throat, and even without looking into a reflective glass, she knew her cheeks would be pinker that she'd like.

How could she not blush? Just the thought that he'd seen and touched her in her nightclothes was enough to make her heart race like a runaway horse. She clasped her hands a little tighter to keep herself from leaping to her feet and hide behind the draperies.

"Your Grace," Lizzy said as soon as Max crossed into the room. "We are so delighted you joined us for tea."

"Mrs. Darcy." Max gave Lizzy a polite nod with his head. He then turned his full attention toward her. "Miss Darcy."

The smile that graced his face was everything she remembered. Both she and Lizzy curtsied and she murmured, "Your Grace."

"Enough of 'Your Grace', please call me Maxwell. We are

all friends here, or at least I hope we are."

"You are most definitely a friend of ours, Maxwell," Lizzy replied. "I know you've asked for a private audience with my sister, but Anna will stay with you while I see cook about tonight's dinner. I won't be longer than fifteen minutes."

She rose to her feet and went to the drawing room door and called Anna to come into the room. Before leaving she gave Georgiana a happy smile and a quick wink. Heat chased across her cheeks once more. What she'd been dreaming of for over three years was about to come true.

Without hesitation Max advanced and sat on the couch beside her. He reached for her hand but for some reason she couldn't relax her fingers, clutched tight in her lap.

"Miss Darcy. Do you fear me?"

"Oh no! How could I?"

"Then will you trust your hand to mine?"

Surprised by the question, her fingers unraveled which allowed him to hold her hand in his. A sensation akin to pins and needles ran up her arm. She'd never had a man touch the bare skin of her hand before, other than family members, and they didn't count. Was this why ladies always wore gloves? To protect them from such intense vibrations?

"Your hands are so cold. Do you wish me to start a fire?"

"No, I am perfectly comfortable, but thank you."

She bit her lip, searching for words. For a way to thank him for saving her.

"I wanted to thank—"

"I came to ask—"

Both stopped mid-sentence. Max spoke first.

"Forgive me Miss Darcy, there is no need to speak of that

situation. I thank God every night that I was there."

"I also thank Him daily. I am afraid I've built you up into knight of the realm proportions."

"Don't place me too high on a pedestal. The fall, when it comes, would be quite painful."

"Very well. I shall make sure the pedestal remains only two feet in height."

Maxwell laughed out loud. "You have a delightful sense of humor."

"Thank you. I blame Lizzy. She has taught me and my brother how to laugh again."

"She brought joy back to Pemberley." Max shifted on the couch and his knee bumped hers. "I requested this time because I have an important question and regardless of what you think you 'should' do, I wish for you to follow your heart." The moment she'd dreaded, yet hoped for, had arrived. "First, I must tell you I have admired you for a number of years. You have grown in grace and beauty and even without these extenuating circumstances, you are someone I have considered as a wife."

An awkward pause stretched before them as he looked at her with expectation. Aware he awaited some form of response, she finally said, "I'm a bit confused. Was there a question in there?"

"Dash it all. I knew I'd forget something." He surprised her by raising her hands to his lips and pressing a soft kiss against her fingers. She absolutely forgot how to breathe. "Yes, there is a question. Would you do me the honor of accepting my hand in marriage? I would have preferred a longer courtship but given the events of this past week your brother wishes to post the banns immediately. Which make sense as the articles of marriage will be ready for signing within the week and the announcement appears in The Gazette tomorrow."

"The announcement will post tomorrow, before the question was asked?" she cried out, withdrawing her hand from Max's light grasp.

She longed to accept his proposal and throw herself into his arms, but no one, absolutely no one had conferred with her about how this would proceed. After everything she'd been through, shouldn't she be given some modicum amount of control in her own fate?

"Miss Darcy, we are not trying to be high-handed in this. Circumstances dictate we move with some haste. Slade is bound for the colonies and cannot spread any vile rumors, but we have no control over the inn keeper or any of his staff and guests. If word, truth or untruth, spread about your harrowing experience, you would be branded a fallen woman and become an outcast."

"I know that." She stood and walked over to the window, wrapping her arms around her midsection. She'd longed for Max to propose, but not under these circumstances. Not because he was forced. Max joined her, standing close but not quite touching. His soothing voice calmed her frustration.

"If you are agreeable to my proposal, we shall have a three-week courtship while the banns are read. More than enough time to allay any rumors which may, or may not arise."

"You do not need to sacrifice your happiness to save my reputation," she managed to breathe out.

"You obviously forgot the first part of my pretty speech. I have always considered you as a woman who could be my

Duchess."

"Always?" She lowered her arms and dared turn around and face him.

He cupped her chin and tilted her face to his. "Always, darling Georgiana."

He leaned in and brushed her lips with his. The kiss, though all too brief, infused her body with heat. When she finally opened her eyes, she found him staring at her, a soft smile on his face.

"Will you marry me, Georgiana Rachel Darcy?"

"Yes. Oh, yes!"

Could the sun shine any brighter? Could her heart expand any further with love?

Max drew her into his arms and laid his forehead against hers. "I shall do my very best to make you happy, sweet girl," he whispered. All too soon, he set her away from him, at arms length. "Now I must go and tell Mother the good news."

"Will you come for dinner tonight?" she asked, marvelling at how calm her voice sounded when every nerve in her body sizzled and popped like a Yule log.

"Would that I could, love, but I shall be quite busy informing family of our good news." He stepped toward her and, unmindful of Anna's presence in the room, kissed her hard on the mouth. "Until tomorrow, Georgiana."

It was only when the door to the room closed behind him that she realized she still stood with trembling fingers touching her lips. Such longing filled her body. A longing for what she did not know, but was assured in her heart that Maxwell completed her like no other person in the world. Her wedding could not come soon enough.

~~~~~

Amber liquid glinted in the light from the fireplace as Max slowly rotated the cut glass tumbler, deep in thought over his upcoming nuptials on the morrow. He raised the brandy to his lips and liquid fire trailed past his tongue and worked its way into his belly, leaving behind a warm glow.

"What?" An exclamation from the direction of the door to his study brought him out of his musings. "Drowning your sorrows already, brother?"

Max smiled as George entered the room, followed closely by Nathan.

"Not drowning. Enjoying a quiet moment before the busyness of tomorrow."

He signaled Hutchins, who remained by the door, to pour each of his brothers a drink and then dismissed him.

"Aye," Nathan said. "When you look back, you'll find you remember only a few key things. The rest of the day is but a blur."

George nodded in agreement. "All I remember is my Catherine walking toward me."

"You both are such romantics," Max teased.

"Laugh now, but I guarantee the minute Georgiana enters the room on her brother's arm everyone in the sanctuary will fade away."

"You may be right, George," Max conceded. "I've waited a long time for this day."

Understanding dawned on George's face and he turned to Nathan. "Georgiana Darcy is the one Max mooned over all these years?"

Nathan nodded and smiled. "From what I've witnessed

firsthand, our eldest brother has quietly admired Miss Darcy for a long time. I'm happy to report she returns his affection."

Satisfaction coursed through Maxwell's body. Knowing Georgiana viewed him in a favorable light bode well for their future. Over the past few weeks, they'd enjoyed many conversations but not once did either of them bring up the tender subject of love.

Circumstances surrounding their hasty engagement and marriage made such conversations difficult. If Nathan's assertations were accurate, their marriage would be felicitous and the intimacies of their union not as awkward as he feared.

A discreet knock at the door announced the arrival of Hutchins.

"Mr. Darcy and Colonel Fitzwilliam, your Grace."

Hutchins stepped to one side, allowing Darcy to enter the room, followed by his cousin.

"Darcy. Fitzwilliam. What brought you here?"

"Too many conversations revolving around lace, flowers, and fripperies," Richard groused, helping himself to a tumbler of brandy after Max waved Hutchins off. "We desperately needed some conversation about dogs, horses, and hunting."

Laughter filled the air and soon all five of them were comfortably ensconced in chairs dotted about the room.

"Are you and Georgiana leaving immediately after the wedding breakfast?" Darcy asked.

"We'll see how the day goes. These past few weeks have been so hectic, Georgiana may wish to spend a few quiet evenings here, near family. As well, I cannot tarry too long with my new bride as I am required to be in the House of Lords. There are some important bills being put forward with all the unrest in the North, and I wish to be here for the vote."

"I wouldn't recommend the Continent. Even with Old Boney surrendering, the whole area is in a state of upheaval," Richard said.

"I thought I may take her on a tour of Scotland."

"My sister would enjoy that. She's always wanted to view some castles and has often expressed an interest in sighting the fabled Loch Ness sea creature."

"She has more chance at a sighting of the Fae," Richard guffawed. "George, do you remember when Adborough declared he'd seen a wood nymph?"

"Yes! I'd forgotten about that."

"I did not say I saw a wood nymph." Max protested.

"Yes, you did," three voices said in unison.

Nathan glanced at all of them, a puzzled expression on his face. "I don't remember that."

"You were still at Eton," George said. "You always came home a week later than the rest of us. If memory serves me correct, which seems to elude my brother, we were at Pemberley, swimming in the lake near the front of the house."

Max leaned back in his chair, enjoying the sense of comradery which permeated the room. He knew they'd have many years of family gatherings, filled with warmth and laughter. Already he pictured golden haired little girls like their mother and dark-haired boys bearing his features gathered around the fireplace Christmas morning. He wanted the timbers of Adborough Hall to shake from all their laughter and joy. And, when Nathan and George joined them with their families, the room would positively burst from happiness.

~~~~~

The wedding day dawned bright and clear. A good omen, Max thought as he paced in a small room nestled beside the main sanctuary. Nathan and George spoke in low tones with their mother. She excused herself and came toward him, hands outstretched. He clasped them in his, then leaned in and kissed her cheek.

"I am so happy for you, Maxwell. I'd begun to despair of you ever taking a wife."

"I'm very much aware of that, Mother, but I did not want to choose someone I couldn't love."

"And you do love Georgiana, yes?" His mother reached up and brushed an unruly lock of hair from his forehead, a soft smile gracing her still beautiful features.

"Yes, mother. I do love her and hope she will come to love me."

"Pish posh," his mother teased and tapped his chest with an elegant finger. "How could she NOT love you?"

"My bride is very young and inexperienced. As you know, a long courtship was denied us. I don't want her to live her life with regret."

"Maxwell Kerr." He grimaced slightly at her soft chastisement. "I have watched Miss Darcy grow into a lovely young woman and could not fail to notice how much she esteems you. If she doesn't love you now, she will soon. Of that, I am sure." Mother rose up on her toes and gave him a light kiss on the cheek. "I shall see you after the ceremony."

With that, she turned and left the room on Nathan's arm. George gave him a small salute and followed them out. Left to his own devices, Max strolled to a window near the back of the room. Partially hidden by a tapestry covered screen, he listened for the arrival of the Archbishop, who would lead him into the sanctuary. His attention was caught by the sight of the Darcy carriage parked on the road. She was here!

~~~~~

"Are you ready?"

Georgiana looked up at Fitzwilliam's voice and nodded, not trusting her voice.

"Then, take my arm and let's not keep your groom waiting."

He extended his elbow and she placed her gloved hand on his forearm. In her other hand she carried a small bouquet of blush pink roses delivered earlier that morning from Max. The fragrant blooms matched the ribbon on her gown which encircled the bodice before falling softly down her back. Her veil, intricately woven with seed pearls and diamonds, was held in place by the Kerr diadem tiara and she wore a single strand of pearls which had been her mother's. Fitz and Lizzy had presented them after dinner last eve and it was one of the few times she'd seen her brother moved to tears.

Everything coalesced into this defining moment. About to marry a man she loved deeply and start a new life made her heart almost burst to overflowing, and it was with this thought she started the long walk down the aisle.

St. George's parish of Hanover Square was filled to overflowing. The wedding may have been short notice but it wasn't very often that a Duke married, so the pews were packed. Fortunately, the wedding breakfast itself was reserved for family members and close friends, the one exception being Aunt Catherine. Still in high dudgeon over Fitz's marriage to

Elizabeth, she had not apologized for her extreme rudeness from over two years ago and therefore was not back in the family's good graces. Although Georgiana was pleased to see Anne seated next to Cousin Richard, smiling broadly at her and Fitz.

Her first glimpse of Maxwell was of him standing regal and proud next to George. The crowd rustled and murmured in anticipation as she walked by and when they reached the alter, Max turned to face her, his expression loving and warm, if not a bit anxious.

Like her, he must be experiencing wedding nerves and it didn't help they were on display in front of London's elite. Throughout the ceremony, her focus remained on Maxwell and she savored every word spoken, binding them together. How lucky she was, to have captured the interest of such a man. Someone who wanted her for herself and not her fortune.

"I now pronounce you man and wife."

It was done, they were married. Max took her hand and lifted it to his lips, smiling as he kissed her silk encased hand.

"Your Grace," he murmured and gave her hand a squeeze.

"Oh, Maxwell. I'm so happy," she whispered before they turned and strode arm in arm to the back of the cathedral.

"Not nearly as happy as I," he whispered back and they stepped into the bright sunlight to the cheers of a small crowd which had gathered outside the church.

Max hurried her down the grand steps to their waiting carriage and helped her settle before joining her. Lizzy and Fitz, both laughing and smiling, came to the carriage door window.

"We shall meet at Matlock House in a few minutes. Aunt Lucinda set aside a suite of rooms for you to freshen up before the wedding breakfast." Darcy reached for Georgiana's hand. "You are absolutely beautiful, Georgiana. Mother and Father would be so proud of you."

"Thank you, Fitz." She felt tears begin to surface and Max quietly handed her a monogrammed handkerchief. She turned tear filled eyes towards her new husband and smiled. "You are the best of husbands."

"I shall always strive to hold that title." Max said before tapping the roof with his cane to signal the driver to move on.

Chapter Ten

The carriage lurched forward and Georgiana propped her hand on the seat to maintain balance. She and Maxwell were leaving the comfortable posting inn they'd repaired to, shortly after the wedding breakfast. By early afternoon they expected to arrive at Adborough Hall, ancestral home of the Kerr family for nearly one hundred and fifty years. If she and Maxwell were blessed with a son, his legacy would continue.

She craned her neck to peek out the window and watched with longing as Maxwell continued to ride Pericles beside the carriage, slightly behind her line of sight. A puzzled frown creased her forehead, again, as she pondered the events which followed what she thought had been a magical, love filled ceremony.

The wedding breakfast had been a jumble of well-wishers and loads of family hugs and there had barely been enough time for her to change into her traveling clothes before she and Maxwell were barreling down London Road toward Yorkshire.

They'd arrived at the inn and the proprietor had escorted to her own bedchamber. At first, nothing about that seemed unusual. In fact, she'd been grateful for the extra time to prepare. A trifle embarrassed, she'd donned the gauzy gown Lizzy helped her purchase. When the modiste had presented the seductive nightgown, she'd been scandalized, but, as Lizzy had said with a secretive smile, Max was her husband and the shyness would fade away as they became comfortable with one other.

However, Max never once darkened the door to her suite of rooms. She had no idea where he'd slept, or how he'd filled his time and she'd finally crawled into the cold bed alone. The next morning, with no maid to assist, as everyone assumed her husband would be a willing lady's maid, she'd struggled with her gown. Thank goodness the serving maid, who'd brought up her breakfast, stayed and helped fasten the many buttons down the back of her gown.

Now, with the sun high in the sky, they approached Adborough Hall. Expecting to see the full complement of staff, domestic and otherwise lining the stairs to greet them, Georgiana was surprised to see no one. Not even the butler and housekeeper. Surely Max would be furious at this blatant sign of disrespect.

The carriage trundled to a stop and a footman leaped off the carriage, opened the door and lowered the small step. He offered his hand and helped her step down. In the meantime, Max had swung of Pericles and handed the horse off to a waiting groom. Without so much as a look backward, he strode up the stairs and the door opened prior to him reaching the last step.

"Welcome back to Adborough Hall, Your Grace."

What Georgiana assumed was the butler gave Max a respectful half bow. Immediately, after Max entered the house, two footmen exited and began off-loading their trunks. Not knowing exactly what she was supposed to do, she lifted her skirts and ascended the stairs. As she made her way through the doorway, the butler said, "Good day, Your Grace."

It took every ounce of self-control to not burst into tears at that small concession of her presence. Her husband continued through the grand foyer and headed for the stairs. Confused by his bizarre behavior she called out, "Maxwell—"

Slowly he turned and glared.

"You will address me as Your Grace."

Her breath caught at his venom laced words. Desperate to know why he was so angry, she swallowed and tried again.

"Your Grace. May I be so bold as to inquire why—"

"No. You have been bold enough to last a lifetime. We are done here, Madam." He turned and ascended the grand staircase, turning to his left at the top.

Georgiana watched his retreating back and suffered the quiet stares of the butler and housekeeper.

"This way, your Grace."

The housekeeper began to walk toward the same staircase Max had disappeared from.

"To where?"

"Your rooms. I'm sure you'd like to change out of your traveling clothes and freshen up."

The furthest thing from her mind at this moment was changing her clothes. Why was Max behaving in so vile a manner? Her mind came up blank. When he discovered her in Slade's room, he'd been so solicitous and their three-week courtship had been the most wonderful time of her life. Although he'd never said the word, she'd been assured she was loved.

As she followed the housekeeper up the stairs, she remembered she had no lady's maid. She also didn't even know the housekeeper's name. They reached the second floor and turned left and stopped in front of a pale-yellow door. The housekeeper removed a key from her chatelain and unlocked the door. It opened to a lovely room with wide bright windows overlooking the back gardens.

"Thank you, Mrs..., I am sorry, I do not know your name."

"Mrs. Howell, your Grace."

"Thank you, Mrs. Howell."

She glanced about the room, noting how elegantly it was furnished. She longed to know which of the doors led to the master's chamber but was embarrassed to ask. Mrs. Howell cleared her throat and Georgiana brought her attention back to the most immediate concern she had.

"I am in need of a lady's maid, Mrs. Howell.

"You had no lady's maid travel with you?" Mrs. Howell sputtered, quickly masking her dismay behind an implacable façade of calmness. "I shall have someone attend you immediately."

"That would be much appreciated." Georgiana paused, unsure how to ask the next question. "Will Max... I mean, will his Grace be dining any time soon?"

"His Grace has asked for his meal to be sent to his rooms."

Georgiana longed to ask more but Mrs. Howell's manner left her in no doubt she would not be forthcoming with any information about her master.

"If that will be all, your Grace, I shall be about my business. The bell pull is by the window curtain. Please ring if you require anything else."

Mrs. Howell gathered her skirts close and swished out into the hall. Georgiana wandered over to the window and gazed out over the rolling landscape. Under any other circumstance her heart would have sung with joy over starting her new life among such beauty, but as it stood, she felt adrift, like an abandoned child's toy boat left to float upon a lake.

Tears flowed, unchecked, obscuring the verdant, pastoral scene. Dimly she heard the hall clock strike the hour. A sob tore from her throat. Truly she was alone. Horribly alone with nowhere to turn.

A tentative knock on the door had her scramble to gain control of her rising hysteria. She dashed her tears away with the back of her hand. It would not do for Max to find her sobbing.

"Enter," she managed to call out.

A young girl, in the uniform of an upstairs maid entered and gave her a quick curtsy.

"I'm Molly, your Grace. I've come to put away your clothes."

"I'm not sure where my trunks are." Her brow creased in confusion. "Has Mrs. Howell assigned a lady's maid, Molly?"

The girl stood, twisting her fingers together. "I'm not sure who that will be, Your Grace. I was told to come and unpack your trunks." She indicated with her hand the small door near the window. "The footmen brought them to your dressing room."

She bobbed a curtsy and hurried to the door, Georgiana following behind. Molly opened the door, revealing her traveling trunk situated in the middle of a good-sized room.

"Molly, do you know where the Duke is?"

"No, your Grace. Mrs. Howell said to tell you a light repast will be waiting for you in the family dining room."

"And where is that?"

"I'll take you. You might get lost if I try and give you directions."

"I'll need some assistance. I cannot reach the buttons in the back of my gown. Are you willing to lend me a hand until a lady's maid arrives?"

"Oh yes, your Grace. I'll have some hot water brought up immediately."

As Georgiana gave herself a quick, but thorough wash, she worried about Max's change in personality. Everything had been wonderful until the wedding breakfast, and then it was as if someone snuffed out a candle and all light left his body and mind.

Other than the few minutes he'd taken for personal needs before leaving Matlock House, they'd almost been tethered to each other. What happened during that time? Had someone spoken against her? She mentally shook her head. Impossible. Everyone at the wedding breakfast held nothing but good wishes for the both of them. If not that, then what?

Molly came out of the dressing room, a light muslin gown over her arm.

"This one's not too wrinkled, your Grace. I can help you dress and then take you to the dining room."

"Yes, that gown will suffice for this evening. If Mrs.

Howell is unable to locate a lady's maid before the morrow, I will require you to press my remaining dresses."

Not for the first time that day she missed her own lady's maid. Anna was not expected to arrive for another fortnight. If she wrote Fitz directly, maybe he would send Anna to Adborough Hall immediately. Right after her meal she'd prepare a letter to post first thing in the morning.

In no time Georgiana presented herself to the dining room and stopped cold in the doorframe. Max, seated at the table, put down his cup of tea and stood.

"I was told you were having your meal in your room."

"I changed my mind."

He sat and signaled the two footmen, standing in silent tribute against the wall, to begin serving them. She took her seat and for her food. The meal, though not grand, was artfully arranged and tasted as good as it looked, and she hated every single minute. For over half an hour, she endured the scraping of their flatware on expensive dishes in solitary silence. Finally, before the dessert dishes were removed, she summoned the courage to speak.

"Adborough Hall is lovely, at least, what I've seen so far."

"I cannot do this." Max pushed back his chair and stood. "I refuse to pretend all is well and feign ignorance. I leave for London tomorrow morning."

"So soon!" She also pushed back her chair and stood. "Am I to stay here, alone?"

"Yes. I shall leave instructions with Chapman and Mrs. Howell."

He threw his napkin onto his plate and strode from the room. A little dazed over what had just occurred, Georgiana fell back into her chair. What in the world would Max feign ignorance of? She went over all the details from the past few days again and came up blank. She could think of nothing to explain his anger.

With nothing to keep her in the dining room, she exited and began wandering down the hall in search of the grand staircase. Turning a corner, she caught sight of Max near the front entrance speaking with the butler and Mrs. Howell.

"Your Grace," she called out.

Max stopped talking, but did not turn around. She picked up her skirts and hurried toward them, determined to make him speak to her. If nothing else, to have him explain why she was being treated as though she had some dread disease. With dismay, she watched Max hand Mrs. Howell a letter and leave without once acknowledging she had called out to him. Although they maintained a stoic demeanor, Georgiana knew the two head servants were dismayed by their master's behavior.

"Maxwell!" she cried out once more, but the heavy door closed with a resounding thud and she halted in her tracks. No one need tell her that Max was not waiting for morning light to leave Adborough Hall. She'd seen a groomsman, with Pericles, waiting on the graveled drive.

The butler, whom Georgiana learned from Molly was called Mr. Chapman, exchanged a telling glance with Mrs. Howell. He spoke quietly to her and giving Georgiana a polite half bow, exited through one of the many doors lining the grand hall.

Mrs. Howell approached and handed her the envelope Max had given her. The envelope was sealed and addressed to:

Her Grace, Duchess of Adborough. Silently, Mrs. Howell moved down the hall and Georgiana was, once again, left to her own devices.

With trembling fingers, Georgiana opened the envelope and began to read.

Madam,

Your seclusion at Adborough Hall can come as no surprise. I have given instruction that you are not to leave the grounds of Adborough alone. You may attend the nearby village of Dorset for purchase of personal needs as well as attend church with no less than your maid and two footmen, and if accompanied by my trusted steward, Mr. Mason, you may visit my tenants.

Upon my return I will determine how we proceed.

Yours, etc.,
Adborough

The letter fluttered out of her fingers. Her whole body grew numb and began to shake. What had she done? What did he mean her seclusion came at no surprise? She sank to the floor, her skirts puddling around her legs in a mass of wrinkles.

~~~~~

Pericles thundered down the graveled drive, matching the dull fury that flowed through Max. How blind he'd been. If he hadn't overheard a conversation between Darcy and Colonel Fitzwilliam, he'd have blindly entered into his marriage bed and been none the wiser. After attending to some personal needs, he'd stopped to adjust a buckle outside the library door at Matlock House and heard the words that broke his heart in two.

"Surely you're happy for Georgie."

"I am. Adborough is an admirable man. My only regret is that this marriage was such a rushed affair."

"Must needs, Richard. We had no guarantee rumors would not spread and I couldn't make this one go away."

"Aye, not like Ramsgate. For some reason he never spoke a word of it to anyone."

"I suppose, in his own way, he cared for her. That may have been the only time he showed discretion in anything."

Max remembered how everything around him faded until all he was aware of was his breathing and the sound of his heartbeat. Nothing else existed. What had Darcy meant by; *I couldn't make this one go away*?

At the time he'd entered the first room he came upon and sat in a dazed stupor. By all accounts, his bride had been compromised before and her family had no intention of telling him. Maybe that had been the plan all along. If he'd found out prior to their nuptials, he could have bowed out gracefully, or extended their courtship until he found out more information. By keeping him in the dark, they assured themselves of Georgiana being safely married and he had no recourse but to stay the course. Divorce was out of the question.

Some of his tension must have transferred itself to Pericles because he broke stride and stomped down with his front hoof. It took a few minutes, but Max soothed the beast, who tossed his head with disdain.

"Easy boy. Forgive my ill humor, we'll stop at the next

inn."

Placated, the horse moved on at his urging and they continued down the road, his four outriders keeping pace. It didn't take long before his thoughts went down a dark tunnel and the conversation between Darcy and Colonel Fitzwilliam.

This was not her first compromise. What of her other folly? Could she have a borne a child from that illicit union? He refused to be cuckolded into accepting another man's bastard. He cast his mind back in an attempt to ascertain when her first compromise occurred. There was a time, in her fifteenth year when she'd practically disappeared from company for a good part of the summer. A scant four years ago, but being very familiar with her family, this was the only time when she could have conceived and bore a child.

He thought of her halting speech and pretty blushes. So demure and proper and it had all been an act. Just like Lady Celeste. Thank the Lord he found out before he'd lain with her and been led on a merry chase. Women had ways to make men think they were innocent and untried. Besotted fool that he was, he'd have believed any lie she spewed about how lucky they were their child was so healthy even though born too early.

His only recourse was to return to London and reside there for the next few months, six at most, to ensure his wife was not carrying Slade's child. The quickening may not take place for months, but one thing about a pregnancy – the belly grew whether the woman wanted it to or not.

At the end of his self-imposed exile he'd attend Adborough Hall and consummate the marriage. This was the only way he could ensure any issue from their joining was his.

However, if the babe was a girl... if all this failed...

He refused to think that far ahead. His heart hurt too much and even now, with all this anger swirling around him like a mad winter storm, divorce was an option he could not and would not consider. Whether he liked it or not, the responsibility for the succession of the Duke of Adborough may fall upon the shoulders of his younger brother George.

Chapter Eleven

In the weeks following Max's abrupt departure, Georgiana had never felt so alone – other than her catastrophic summer after Ramsgate. At that time her exile was self-imposed. She'd kept to her room, barely speaking to anyone. It was only with the timely arrival of Mrs. Annesley that she'd finally crawled out of the dark abyss her mind had fallen into. And now, as she wandered the grounds of Adborough Hall, with a silent footman following at a discreet distance, her mind turned to the advice her faithful companion had given her. Put her thoughts down onto paper.

Mrs. Annesley's recommendation had carried her through those difficult months and would do so again. So, quill in hand, she sat down at her escritoire to do the same with regard to Maxwell. At first, she struggled to gather her thoughts, but within minutes it was as though the floodgates of her heart opened and the words poured onto the pages.

~~~~~

"Lord Nathan, Ma'am,"

Startled, Georgiana looked up from the book she'd been reading. Oblivious to her surroundings, caught up in the world of the Miss Dashwood's, she hadn't heard a carriage.

After carefully placing an embroidery thread within the pages of the book to mark her place, she set it down on the side table and stood to smooth her skirts. Not counting the arrival of her maid Anna, along with all her trunks and personal belongings from Pemberley, this was the first time anyone had paid a visit.

Lord Nathan entered the room and without preamble, advanced toward her taking both hands in his. He kissed her gently on the cheek, saying, "You look lovely as always, Georgiana. Caroline sends her love and regrets that she could not attend with me."

She looked toward the door and caught the butler's attention when Lord Nathan released her hands. "Please have Cook send up a tray of tea and biscuits."

"Right away, Ma'am." Chapman replied.

"Ask if she has any pear tarts," Nathan interjected, a happy grin creasing his face. "I absolutely love Dawson's pear tarts."

"I shall see if she has any, Master Nathan," Chapman said with a slight smile before bowing out of the room.

"Please, have a seat Lord Nathan." She sat and settled her skirts around her legs. "I didn't hear your carriage."

"That is because I arrived by horseback. Also, now that you are my sister, you must call me Nathan. How did you get that bruise on your forehead?"

"This?" Georgiana touched the small wound which had almost faded completely. "Tis nothing but the result of a small fall." She had no desire to inform him how a tenant had pushed by her in anger during one of her visits with Mr. Mason. The steward had apologized profusely, as had the tenant.

Nathan sat directly across from her and took note of the book on the side table. "I see you are reading *Sense & Sensibility*. Caroline and Catherine are as well."

"Are they? I shall have to correspond with them and find out what they think of the dastardly Mrs. John Dashwood."

"That's partly why I'm here."

"You wished to discuss Mrs. John Dashwood?"

"No." He chuckled softly. "Caroline has not heard from her dear friend, the Duchess of Adborough in ages – her words, not mine – and I was tasked to find out if you are vexed with her for some reason."

"I am not." She hesitated, unsure of how to explain her circumstances without putting herself into a bad light. "I've been busy settling in, becoming familiar with Adborough Hall."

"I'm sure Maxwell has been as proud as a peacock, showing you all the rooms and taking you on a tour of the grounds. That would explain why we haven't heard from him either."

"I... that is to say... his Grace is not here."

Her bottom lip trembled and she fought to keep her tears at bay. She would not cry in front of him, she just wouldn't. Max would never forgive her. She turned her face to the window, willing her emotions into a semblance of calm.

"May I ask where, exactly, my brother is? I'm assuming, given your unhappiness, he is not within the vicinity of Adborough Hall," Nathan asked, his voice deceptively calm.

"No, he is not." She took a deep breath and faced him. "He

is in London."

"And when did he leave for London?"

"The evening we arrived."

"The same day—!" Nathan stood and marched to the drawing room door. "Chapman!" he called out. Within seconds the butler appeared.

"Yes, my Lord?"

"Do you have any clear idea why my brother has abandoned his wife?"

"I am not at liberty to speak about this matter, my Lord."

"Not at liberty to speak about this matter with anyone, or just Lady Maxwell Kerr?"

"Lady Maxwell Kerr, my Lord."

"Nathan, please." Georgiana stood, twisting her fingers in agitation. "Do not blame Mr. Chapman. I'm sure he is only following His Grace's instructions. He said as much in his letter to me."

"His letter?" Nathan whipped around. "I would very much like to see this letter and while you are fetching it, I will have a talk with Mr. Chapman."

"I don't…" she began. Nathan leveled a 'do not prevaricate with me' look at her. "Very well."

She eased by the two men, noticing how uncomfortable Mr. Chapman seemed to be and also how he avoided looking directly at her. She regretted mentioning Max's letter and wished she'd consigned the hateful thing to the fire, but she hadn't and now Nathan would know her shame.

Upon entering her suite of rooms, she opened her desk and found the letter nestled in the pages of her Bible. Other than putting her thoughts on paper, reading the Book of Psalms had become her other source of comfort. She took great solace in the assurance that if God would protect King David in his time of trouble, He'd look after her in her time of sorrow.

She returned to the drawing room in time to see Mr. Chapman and Mrs. Howell both exiting. At seeing her, they stopped and waited respectfully for her to pass by. Lord Nathan stood by the fireplace, staring into the flames, his back to her. At the sound of her skirts rustling, he turned around, anger etched into every crevice of his face. Without a word, he held out his hand and she placed the letter in it.

As he read the short missive, a vein began to pulse at his temple and his lips thinned to an angry, straight line. In all the years she'd known Lord Nathan, she'd never seen him furious and hoped to high heaven she never would again. Finally, with exaggerated care, he folded the letter and handed it back to her.

"I must take my leave." He spoke as though he chose his words carefully. "Please know I am appalled by my brother's behavior and hold you in the highest regard. Given my discussion with Mr. Chapman and Mrs. Howell my brother has a lot of explaining."

"Will you not stay to dinner? I'd hate to see you leave so soon."

"If I wish to make London by tomorrow night, I must leave now." Lord Nathan gave her a brotherly hug. "I shall check on you again, Georgiana. You are not alone in this anymore."

Before she could mount a protest, or beg him to take her with him, he'd left the room and shortly after she heard his horse thunder down the graveled drive. His hug was the first real human contact she'd had since arriving at Adborough Hall.

~~~~~

"I'll let myself in, Jenkins. Don't bother with tea, I'm not staying long."

Max rose to his feet, a ready smile in place for his brother, but when Nathan flung open the door and glared at him, he clamped his lips tight.

"Who do you think you are?" Nathan punctuated each word with a step forward into the room until he stood directly in front of Max, his hands clenching and unclenching. "You dare to chastise me or George for our previous behavior when you are the worst of us all."

"I have no idea what you are going on about."

Max took a careful step back and moved toward the fireplace. Nathan had a quick temper and an equally quick fist and he had no desire to experience either of them.

"Georgiana."

Max shoulders straightened and all his muscles tightened in response to her name.

"What about… her?" He couldn't bring himself to say her name or call her his wife.

"Her? You refer to your bride as 'her'?"

"Very well, what about my wife?" Bile rose in his throat at that word which by all accounts should signify a loving partner in a loving marriage. Neither of which he enjoyed.

"Are you sure she's your wife? You've treated her worse than a harlot. You abandoned her at Adborough Hall, creating a scurrilous rumor that she may be pregnant by another man and ordered your staff to keep a watchful eye on her belly to see if it grows with child. You have subjected her to an embarrassing scrutiny for reasons she has no knowledge of."

Nathan's words brought on a swell of resentment in his

chest.

"Be careful what you say, brother. You have no right to barge in here—"

"No right? I have no right to tell you that a loving Christian husband honors his wife? That he lays down his life for her as Christ laid down His for us? As your brother and a former vicar of the Church of England, I have no right to tell you to remove the beam from your eye before you attempt to remove logs from another's?"

"No, you do not." Max clasped his hands behind his back and held his gaze steady. Nathan had no idea what he'd gone through after his marriage to Georgiana. How his heart had been ripped apart at the thought of her being intimate with not one man, but two.

"Your wife sits alone in a large, unfamiliar house with no one to take care of her. She wouldn't tell me how her face became bruised—"

"Her face? What happened?" Max's heart lurched at the thought of Georgiana being injured.

"Now you show concern! If you were by your wife's side, you'd know one of the tenants shoved her during one of her visits."

"My staff said nothing of this."

"Maybe they are taking their lead from you and think your wife is not worthy of any show of warmth, or compassion." Nathan jeered. "At my insistence, Chapman divulged what had occurred. Thankfully, she required no stitches." Nathan paced to the window and back. "What is going on in your mind? I cannot, for the life of me, fathom a reason for you to behave in this manner?"

"You have no idea what I've endured in all of this, of what I know."

"What *you've* endured?" Nathan scoffed; his voice filled with contempt.

"I'm not her first lover."

There he'd said it. Voiced the very words that twisted his gut night after night.

"Do you know this for an absolute fact?"

"Yes. Slade was not her first compromise, there was another."

"Did you think to speak to your wife about this information, seeing as it concerns her?"

"I could not. It was like Constance Templeton all over again seeking an idiot to believe another man's bastard was his own child."

"My god! This is what you think of Georgiana. A girl you've known from infancy?" Nathan stepped away from him and moved to the front of the desk. "For your information, your wife in not enceinte."

The tight band around his chest lessened at the news. Upon seeing the relief etched across his face, Nathan spat out. "May God have mercy on you, Maxwell, because at this very moment I have none. My heart is filled with sorrow. Caroline and I will pray for you. It's all that we can do, but until you reconcile with your wife and beg her forgiveness, you are not welcome at Moreland Park."

With those words, Nathan left the room, closing the door behind him with a quiet click. Max almost wished he'd slammed the door because then he could justify to himself that his brother had acted irrationally.

~~~~~~

Three days later…Pemberley

The clock had finished marking the ninth hour and the scratching of a quill was the only sound in Darcy's study when his butler announced, "Lord Nathan Kerr, sir."

Surprised, Darcy deposited the quill into the ink pot and stood. Before he could move around the desk to greet Nathan, his previous vicar entered the room, clearly agitated and clearly exhausted.

"Kerr, what brings you here this time of night?"

"I regret I have to inform you of something quite serious regarding Georgiana."

"Sit down." Darcy waved Nathan toward the chairs by the fireplace. "Carson, see if Cook can prepare some food as I'm sure Lord Nathan has not yet eaten this evening, and have Mrs. Reynolds prepare a room."

"Yes, sir."

"What is this all about?" Darcy sat in one of the chairs. "What about Georgiana?"

"On my way to London, I stopped by Adborough Hall to pay my respects." He leaned forward and with elbows on his knees, clasped his hands together. "Caroline had become worried because she'd not heard one word from neither Georgiana or Max."

"They've been on their wedding trip. They were taking a tour through Scotland." Darcy interjected.

"They did not go on any wedding trip." Nathan sat fully back into his chair. "My brother took your sister, his wife, to Adborough Hall immediately following the wedding breakfast and then returned to London. Alone."

"He what!" Darcy stood and began to pace. "Tell me everything."

For the next half hour, Nathan proceeded to inform him how Georgiana has been alone at Adborough Hall. The more questions Darcy asked, the more enraged he became. He reached his boiling point when Nathan said, "Your sister has no knowledge the housekeeper and senior staff have been informed to see if she is increasing."

"Georgiana's pregnant already? Does your brother intend to return in time for the birth of his child?"

"No…" Nathan hesitated ever so slightly. "They are to ascertain if she was increasing with Sir Reginald Slade's child."

"Slade's child!" Darcy clenched his hand, wishing he could strike out at the man whom he trusted with his sister's well being. "He thinks Georgian was violated by that snake in the grass?"

"He knows this is not the first time Georgiana has been compromised and therefore is unsure if she's a maiden, or if she willingly went with Slade."

"That son of a… Forgive me, Kerr. I hold your mother in the highest esteem and lost my head for a moment."

"Darcy, this is none of my business, but I must ask and you can be assured your answer will never leave my lips, not even to my wife. Is Max wrong in the assessment this was not her first compromise?"

"No." Darcy flung himself into his vacated chair and dragged a hand through his hair. "God help me, I wish I could say otherwise." He straightened. "She was not yet fifteen and staying at Ramsgate with her new governess. George Wickham was there as well and convinced her they were in love. A few days before they were to elope, I arrived at Ramsgate. Needless to say, the affair was cut short before anything happened. Later, my cousin Richard and I discovered the governess was in league with Wickham to swindle my sister out of her dowry. Georgiana was devastated. Wickham was someone she trusted, having known him from the time she was but a child."

"Poor girl."

"It was a difficult period for us all. But, how did your brother find out about all this. The only person I've ever told is Elizabeth and she would never divulge Georgiana's secret."

"I do not know. My conversation with Maxwell didn't progress that far. He's quite convinced that he is the injured party in all of this. None of us knew he was in London, he's obviously trying to keep all of this quiet, which could be an advantage to Georgiana."

"How so?"

"When they return to Society, no one will know what has transpired these past few months. The staff at Adborough Hall are loyal and will not gossip."

"I, for one, don't give a rat's ass if they gossip." Darcy rose to his feet, determined to bring Georgiana home to Pemberley. "Richard arrives tomorrow and will accompany me to Adborough Hall. We will bring Georgiana home."

"If Max digs his heels in, you could be in for quite the fight. He may demand his rights as a husband to have her returned. The House of Lords very likely will fall in his favor and your uncle, Lord Matlock may be squeezed in the middle."

Darcy leaned forward in his chair and held Lord Nathan's gaze. With deadly sincerity he said, "Your brother, if he chooses to put up a fight, will find that my pockets are deep and I have no interest in politics. He can rant and rave all he wants. My sister shall divorce him and that will be the end of it. She need never marry so it does not matter if there is a scandal."

"Darcy, before you become my brother's judge and executioner, I'd err on the side of caution. Georgiana may not *need* to marry again, but she may *want* to marry again, or stay married. Need I remind you how much she loves Maxwell? She has a right to make her own choice this time around, seeing as she didn't have one before."

"I forgot what a persuasive man you are Kerr. However, I am still taking Richard to Adborough Hall and we will 'discuss' what transpires next, but I cannot guarantee that I won't push to have her return to Pemberley where she is loved beyond reason."

Chapter Twelve

"Georgiana!"

At the sound of her brother's voice, Georgiana dropped the quill onto her journal, leapt to her feet and began running as fast as she could down the long hall from her suite of rooms. She practically flew down the stairs and met him at the bottom. He stood, his arms wide, and she fell into them. For so many months she'd been alone, and scared. Fitzwilliam brought with him a sense of familiarity and love. Something she now realized she needed as much as food and air. She squeezed her arms tighter, not wanting to leave this cocoon of safety.

"Sister, I have need of air and if you squeeze any harder, I might collapse and then Richard will never let me forget this."

"He's right, Georgiana. Although I'm feeling rather lonely over here with no hug."

Reluctantly, she stepped out of her brother's embrace and acknowledged her cousin with a smile. In her haste to greet her brother she hadn't seen Richard standing slightly behind him.

"I'm afraid I was so happy to see my brother I became like

a horse with blinders on. Will you forgive me?"

"Of course, although there is nothing to forgive." Richard came forward and gave her a quick kiss on the cheek.

"I'm a terrible hostess." She turned and spotted Chapman, standing a few feet away. "Have Mrs. Howell prepare a few rooms for my brother and—"

"We will not need any rooms, Georgiana." Darcy cut her off, his face darkening with anger. "We have no intention of spending the night in this house."

"But you've only just arrived."

"We've come to take you home, Georgie." Richard said. "Have your maid pack a trunk."

"Home? What do you mean, take me home?" Her mind couldn't wrap itself around what her cousin was saying. "I'm a married woman. Max has not given me permission to leave."

Fitz quit his angry pacing and gave her a hard look.

"Permission?" he queried. "What do you mean by permission?"

"He... I was told..." she fumbled for words, shame coursing through her body. "Before his Grace left for London, he put down precise instructions in a letter."

A dark silence stretched between brother and sister, broken by a quiet request.

"May I see the letter, Georgiana?"

Her shame knowing no boundaries, she nodded and hurried to her room, returning with the letter in hand. Fitz thanked her and removed himself to the window to read the hated missive. Slowly, his hand crumpled the sheet of paper. Ironically, she almost cried out to stop. It was the only letter Max had ever written her and for some unknown reason she wished to keep it.

Fitz finally faced her and, with a muscle twitching in his cheek, gave Richard a telling look. His gaze cut to Chapman, who remained nearby in stoic silence.

"While my sister packs her trunk, I will have a word with you and – he glanced at the crumpled letter – Mrs. Howell. Have a man prepare a carriage for my sister and her maid."

Chapman gave him a polite half bow and disappeared through one of the servant's doors.

"Run along now, Georgie and gather a few things. We'll have someone send the rest of your belongings after you are at Pemberley."

Fitz turned to Richard and began to talk quietly.

"No."

Both men looked at her in surprise.

"Pardon?" Fitz asked.

"You expect me to meekly scurry off to my room and pack my bags without one word of explanation?"

"Georgie... it's complicated and now is not the time to discuss things. I'd like to reach the posting inn before it's too dark to ride safely."

"No." Tired of being told one way or another what she could or could not do, she finally held her ground.

"No?" Both Fitz and Richard spoke the word.

"I am not moving from this spot until someone tells me what has been going on."

Darcy threw a helpless look at Richard who only shrugged his shoulders. Silent communication travelled between the two cousins and Georgiana envied their long friendship. Would that she had anyone who knew her so intimately.

"You've got to tell her, Darce." Richard finally said.

"This conversation should be away from listening ears." Fitz waved an arm toward one of the front parlors. "Before we have this conversation, please have your maid begin packing your trunk."

"No, Fitzwilliam. I will hear what you have to say and *then* I'll make the decision as to whether I stay or go."

Her brother assessed her quietly. "You look and sound so much like Mother it's quite frightening."

"That's one of the nicest things you've ever said to me." Her throat tightened with emotion.

"It's true, Georgie. Your mother was a fearsome woman to behold when she fought for what she thought was right. The battles she had with Aunt Catherine were epic." Richard reminisced with a smile.

"If that is the case, gird your loins because I am demanding to be treated as a woman, not a child."

With that, she gathered her skirts and sailed into the parlor, her brother and cousin falling in behind. For the first time in months she felt a surge of confidence. Once she knew why Maxwell had abandoned her so soon after their wedding, she could set about to repair the damage and they could begin again. Surely it was only a misunderstanding. She settled herself in an elegant brocade chair and waited for Fitz and Richard to stop prowling around the room like two caged tigers. Finally, her brother stopped pacing and faced her.

"I hate to ask such personal questions but there are some things I must know in order to proceed."

"Ask me anything, brother. I have nothing to hide."

"Have you lain with Adborough?"

"Lain with him?" she repeated back, wondering why her brother would ask such a question. "I don't understand what that has to do with anything."

"We need to know if you and Adborough have been intimate, Georgie," Richard offered by way of explanation. "If he's shown you any increased affection."

"He has kissed me." She twisted her fingers together in agitation and knew her cheeks were pinkened by embarrassment. "I'll ask you again. What does this have to do with anything?"

Fitz sat in the chair next to her, leaned over and took her hand in his.

"Adborough believes Slade may have fully compromised you and at this time you may be carrying his child. If you were, he'd proceed to have the child taken care of and only then would he consummate the marriage with you in order to ensure any progeny was his, and his alone."

"He believes I may be with child?"

Dumbfounded, Georgiana stared, open-mouthed at her brother and cousin. How could Max believe she'd been intimate with Sir Reginald. He himself had seen she was still in her nightgown. Something else must have happened.

"There's more to this, Georgiana," Fitz said, his voice sounding almost weary. He stood and paced from the window to the fireplace and back to the window, twisting his pinky ring. Something he did when extremely nervous, which was not very often. He turned to speak and stopped, giving a helpless look toward Richard. That was when she knew what he wanted to say was not good. In fact, it could be very bad, indeed.

Richard took over. "Adborough knows about Ramsgate."

She gasped.

"We don't know how he knows, and he does not have all the facts, but he put two and two together and came up with six. That's the reasoning behind his decision to leave you here until he knew, without a shadow of doubt, you are not with child."

Georgiana let the words sink in. Instead of having a conversation with the woman he was going to spend the rest of his life with, he'd chosen to believe the worst. She lifted her chin with determination. He'd chosen wrong. No longer would she allow others to dictate her actions and pass judgement when she made errors. Today she took back her own life. Today she became her own woman. She rose to her feet. Fitz stopped pacing and Richard remained very still.

"Please give Anna and me an hour to pack. I will meet you in the front foyer."

~~~~~

Georgiana hurried down to the music room to retrieve her sheets of music. She passed her maid in the hall, her arms full of linens.

"Is that the last of my belongings?"

"Yes, my Lady. I'll be done shortly and have a footman bring down the trunk right away.

"Thank you, Anna. I'll be waiting in the front foyer when you are ready."

Anna hurried down to Lady Georgiana's room and quickly placed the last bits of clothing in the waiting trunk. About to exit the now empty bedchamber, she spied a package of letters on her ladyship's desk. She picked them up and saw they were addressed to His Grace, The Duke of Adborough. Before she retrieved her cloak, she bundled them up with a pale pink ribbon and placed them in the box for outgoing mail near the butler's office. Mr. Chapman would see that they were forwarded to the Duke tomorrow morning.

Georgiana slid the sheets into a leather folder made especially for her music and hurried into the front foyer. Chapman waited by the door; her cloak folded over his arm. Anna slipped into the room through a servant's door.

"Anna, I think I left some letters on my desk. Did you take care of them?"

She'd written a final letter before leaving. It somehow seemed fitting, but couldn't recall if she'd placed them with her new journal for packing.

"Yes, m'Lady." Anna said. "I made sure they were all tied together so they wouldn't become separated and lost."

"Good." Her shoulders slumped in relief. She did not want Mrs. Howell or one of the other maids to inadvertently come across them. They might take it upon themselves to read them and have a good laugh over what a foolish girl she'd been. In fact, she should burn them, but there wasn't time. Fitz was pacing the entrance way as it was and Richard had assumed a silent vigil near the front door.

Georgiana shrugged the cloak over her shoulders and with a quick glance toward Chapman, she whispered a thank you. He acknowledged her with a slight, yet gracious nod. The carriage trundled up the drive from the stables. She and Anna would ride together, while Fitz and Richard rode alongside with the armed outriders. She hurried down the front steps of

Adborough Hall and was helped into the carriage by a young footman. Although his face remained stoic, Georgiana could see that his eyes were full of curiosity.

Her escape had all the elements of a Gothic novel. Courageous heroine stealing away with her maid before the evil master returned. At least the sun shone bright and she wasn't in her nightgown, trussed up in a smelly woolen blanket. A small part of her acknowledged this time Maxwell would not be her knight in shining armor. After three long months with no word from him and learning what he believed of her, she held no hope of his return.

Two days later...London

"These arrived by post this morning, your Grace." Benson carefully placed the mail on the corner of his desk.

Max looked up from his desk where he'd been unsuccessfully trying to balance the household accounts from Adborough Hall. This was madness, attempting to run his estate from London. What would take only an hour or two with his steward now took weeks. On top of that he couldn't stop thinking of the visit Nathan paid him over a week ago, levelling all sorts of accusations.

Since then he'd spent many restless nights vacillating between anger and heartache. Angered by how deceived he'd been and heartache over the lost dream of a girl he'd love for so long. Even if he returned to Adborough Hall after the self-imposed exile, he didn't know if he could bear becoming intimate with a woman who had known other men.

He eyed the usual pile of envelopes and stopped breathing

at the sight of a stack of ivory cream ones emblazoned with his ducal crest, bound by a soft pink ribbon.

With a mixture of anger and trepidation Max stared at them for over ten minutes. Convinced they would be endless pleas for forgiveness coupled with Georgiana begging to be allowed to attend London so she could snare another unsuspecting dupe into fawning over her, he tossed them into a drawer.

Two weeks later, searching for a ledger, Max stopped cold as his hand pushed against the bundle of letters. Anticipating a return of his anger, yet knowing he should read the blasted things, he slid the ribbon off and opened the first letter.

September 16, 1814

My darling Maxwell,

May I call you Maxwell, for that is how I think of you? Forgive me for being so forward, but Mrs. Annesley long ago advised me to write down what is close to my heart when I cannot speak them with my mouth — and you are my heart.

I have loved you for as long as I can remember and the thought of you being in London, angry with me, breaks me in two. I fear the unknown and the reason for your cold, cold wrath.

How I wish you would return to Adborough Hall. I miss your voice, your laughter, sure to erupt when Sir Waddlesworth skids on Mrs. Howell's polished marble floors. He is a fluffy white cat I have befriended. I miss the very presence of you in each room. However, if wishes were horses, you'd have a stable full of thoroughbreds and I can't make you come home.

Instead, I will tell you what has been happening since you've gone.

Mrs. Dawson has chased poor Sir Waddlesworth out from the kitchen three times this week. He has such a weakness for kippers and who can blame him, for he is a cat. Mr. Powell continues to prune the shrubs and trees, and the trees are a glorious riot of color. I have pressed a few leaves into my memory book. This will be my first fall as the Duchess of Adborough and I wish to create something for our children to remember.

I cannot write anymore. The page will be soaked through if I continue to write while I cry like a child. Forgive me. I love you. I miss you. I ask your forgiveness for whatever I've done.

Georgiana Kerr

Max laid the letter down on his desk and deep-seated anger bubbled up from his core. How could she write such loving words? Did she think he'd come galloping back like a lovesick fool to Adborough Hall, all because she wrote a few pretty sentences?

He slammed his hand over the letter on the desk and stood. How could he forgive her, when the lies she and her brother withheld had broken his trust? He slid the letters into the top drawer of his desk, locked it and left the room. A brisk ride through Hyde Park would clear his head.

It was two long days before he returned to her letters.

September 18, 1814

My darling Max,

Yesterday I was filled with reservation that writing down my feelings would make me feel better, but today I awakened with renewed hope. Why did I ever doubt Mrs. Annesley? She has been such a good mentor and I would dearly love to see her again, if only to ask for some much-needed guidance.

Putting my thoughts down on paper has given me more clarity with regard to this estrangement. It's almost as if my cloudy reasoning has been swept away like pesky cobwebs in the attic. I recall Mrs. Reynolds saying that my mother kept a journal and I now see the benefits. I believe on my next journey to the village I will order one from London. Pray, don't worry of the expense. I have plenty of pin money as I do not go anywhere or see anybody — other than Sir Waddlesworth. He has become my faithful, if somewhat silent, companion.

Your head steward, Mr. Mason, brought to my attention the Bothwell family. They've had a touch of influenza in their household. Mrs. Dawson prepared a nice broth with some fresh bread and I visited them this morning. Mrs. Bothwell was so receptive. I didn't feel too nervous, but then I'm used to visiting tenants at Pemberley. Mrs. Bothwell mentioned a few other tenants are having some difficulty with their roofs as well minor sickness so I hope you don't mind, but I spoke with Mr. Mason and he rode out immediately to ascertain what they required.

Thankfully, only two families had the same influenza symptoms and Mr. Mason is taking a few men with him to patch up the roofs which sustained water damage. I shall visit the other families on the morrow.

I love you and I miss you.

Georgiana Kerr

Max read through the letter again. The first time she'd

written that she loved him had pierced his heart. Did she even know what love was? Everything in him screamed she was being manipulative even though his bruised heart wanted to believe every last word. Why else would she write so openly about love? Not once, during their whirlwind courtship, had she ever given voice to how she felt, although he'd believed it implied by her actions. This was so completely out of character. Something didn't ring true.

A quick glance at the date showed she'd written this letter in September, almost two months after he'd returned to London and a month before Nathan confronted him. Why were her letters so outdated?

Chapter Thirteen

"Georgiana, do you wish to join me? Bennet and I are going for a short ramble through the woods," Elizabeth Darcy called through the door. Georgiana didn't even bother to lift her head from the pillow upon which she lay before answering in the negative.

"Very well, but please join us for dinner tonight. We want you to live your life again, dearest."

Live her life again. For what purpose?

Georgiana turned on to her side and burrowed her face into the pillow. She'd been at Pemberley for almost a month and still no correspondence or sign of Maxwell. Not even a letter from his solicitor telling her that he was extremely sorry but he didn't want to be married to her anymore. And it had been four months since she'd watched him ride away from Adborough Hall. She flipped onto her back and stared at the filmy lace bordering the canopy of her bed.

Such frippery, chosen when she was but a child, all fluffy

and lacy, and pink, and stupid— She jumped off the bed and began ripping at the lace. Anna entered the room and stopped cold.

"Your Grace——" she began.

"I am not your Grace!" Georgiana whirled around and faced her maid, tattered lace clenched in her fists. "I am nothing. I am nobody. I am unloved and unwanted." She fell to the floor, choking sobs pummeling her frail body.

"I'll get Mrs. Darcy." Anna spun around and dashed down the hall, calling out, "Mrs. Darcy. Mrs. Darcy, come quick. It's Miss Darcy, I mean it's her Ladyship."

Through her retching sobs, Georgiana dimly heard Elizabeth rush into the room and soon her soothing voice cut through all the agonized clutter that filled her mind and dreams.

"Shh.... Georgie. Shh.... Come here, dearest."

Elizabeth gathered Georgiana in her arms and rocking her gently, stayed seated on the floor with her until the sobbing finally subsided. With a shuddering breath, Georgiana hugged Elizabeth around her ever thickening waist.

"I am so sorry, Lizzy. I am so sorry."

"What do you have to be sorry about?" Elizabeth caressed her back with long comforting strokes. Georgiana recognized this as the same method in which Lizzy settled young Bennet when he had a crying fit, and though she was a married woman, she didn't mind the cossetting. When she'd settled, Elizabeth moved away slightly and with one finger beneath her chin, raised her tear stained face to hers.

"Now tell me. What do you have to be sorry about?" She clasped her hands on her lap, and although they were both sitting on the floor in a wrinkled pile of skirts, she managed to look regal. Not for the first time Georgiana wished she could emulate the strength of character Lizzy had.

"I have failed at my marriage. My husband cannot bear to be in the same room with me let alone a gigantic estate, and I am sure he will divorce me once he discovers I left Adborough Hall against his express wishes."

The only sign of Lizzy's anger was a slight pursing of her lips.

"Your husband has much to answer for, but you defying his orders and leaving Adborough Hall is not one of them."

"Maybe I should have stayed and waited until he returned. He did say he'd come back in six months and that's only two months away. If I'd have waited—"

"Georgiana," Lizzy interrupted angrily. "I do not care what Society might dictate in circumstance such as these. He had no right to abandon you based on an overheard conversation. He promised to keep you safe and give you a loving home."

"If I had a candy drop for every broken promise I've received in my life, my jar would overflow," Georgiana whispered into Lizzy's shoulder.

"Oh, sweetling," Lizzy gave her another tight hug before rising to her feet with Georgiana's help. "Do not be so hard on yourself. When you feel this low, you can only go up, and Fitzwilliam and I shall endure the climb with you."

~~~~~

September 30, 1814

My darling Maxwell,

How familiar that phrase has become to me. I'm sure when you return home, I will make a mistake and blurt it out. I can only imagine how surprised you'd look if I uttered those three little words, or the fact that I love you — most faithfully — upon your arrival.

It's been almost two weeks since I last wrote. I took some preserves, along with soup and bread to the other two families with illness. I'm so glad I did. The father of the one family was quite incapacitated and in such a weakened state. I'm sure the broth will do him good. I've instructed Mr. Mason to give them a few hens for eggs.

Sir Waddlesworth is quite pleased with himself. He managed to catch a mouse near the stables. Imagine my horror when he proudly presented it to me in the front parlor. I thought Mrs. Howell was going to have an apoplectic fit, but she managed to smile through clenched teeth and only give him a light scolding. Honestly, Maxwell, I thought she was going to fall on the floor, she turned so red.

As of this afternoon, Sir Waddlesworth is banished to the stables, for which he's miserable but it keeps Mrs. Howell happy. I shall miss his gentle purring. He would visit me in the night and curl up near my feet. His warm little body was comforting and I didn't feel so alone.

I love you and I miss you,

Georgiana Kerr

Max carefully laid the letter on his desk and vacillated between feeling a sense of satisfaction with how Georgiana had jumped into her duties as mistress of Adborough Hall and a sense of guilt over her perceived loneliness where she had only a stray cat for companionship. She had so many redeeming qualities it tore at his conscious that he couldn't be assured of her fidelity... and yet she didn't behave as someone who'd done wrong.

Did she get a restful sleep or did she toss and turn at night like him? In the quiet hours when nothing could be heard except the steady ticking of the grandfather clock, his conscience poked at his motives for leaving Georgian alone. Not once in any of the letters he'd read so far had she beg him to return, or request her presence with him in London. Instead, she showed remarkable fortitude and a stoicism he could respect.

He picked up the next letter and began to read.

October 4, 1814

My darling Maxwell,

You've been gone nearly three months without any word on when you'll return. My heart aches. It's like a physical pain in my chest and I can scarce breath when I think of you. Last night I cried myself to sleep after remembering our waltz at George and Kitty's wedding ball.

When you held me in your arms and whirled me around the ball room I felt as though I had wings. Everything and everybody melted away leaving only you and I, and how I wished you had kissed me then. I'm sure it would have been magical, just as it was when you finally kissed me at the Featherstone ball. You were my first and last kiss for all eternity.

Did you know I fell in love with you when I was but sixteen? You'd come to visit Nathan prior to Fitzwilliam's wedding and stayed to dinner. Most people ignored me, as I was so painfully shy, but you made the effort to include me. I'd never noticed that before, but you always treated me as a young lady ought to be treated.

Not many people know this, but a few months prior to my

fifteenth birthday a close family friend ingratiated himself with my governess. The two of them conspired to make me fall in love with him, at which time he planned to whisk me away to Gretna Green and we would marry. I was so naïve and believed all his serpentine lies. How could I know the only incentive for him was my substantial dowry? Thankfully, I'd written my brother and he arrived in time to save my honor and my reputation.

One day, when we're old and gray and I'm assured of your undying love, I may tell you all about George Wickham. He is a chapter of my life I never want to repeat and if we ever have a daughter, I will make sure she is aware of the pretty tales desperate men tell young foolish girls who read too many romance novels. You will have very intelligent daughters, Maxwell – after I've given you at least three healthy sons to carry on the Kerr name, much like you and your handsome brothers.

I love you and I miss you.

Georgiana Kerr

Max threw the letter down and stood, not sure if he wanted to ride out and find Wickham to call him out, or head straight to Adborough Hall and tell Georgiana how sorry he was that he doubted her sincerity.

For years he'd admired her gentle manners and shy demeanor. He adored the fact that she brightened when he entered a room. He always knew it was because she felt safe with him and given what he knew now, it explained so much. He remembered telling Nathan, '*It's as though she's had great sorrow in her life and from that sorrow, she sees the world for what it is. Not all rose gardens and parties.*'

He also remembered the waltz, the way she fit perfectly

in his arms tucked right next to his heart, the light scent of honeysuckle perfume tickling his nose. It had taken every ounce of his will power not to whisk her out of the ball room and beg her to marry him. The thought of having children with Georgiana created an aching void where his heart once hung. How could she ever forgive him for his boorish pride?

He returned to his desk and with trembling hands, picked up the next letter.

October 14, 1814

My darling Maxwell,

I have just finished re-reading Sense and Sensibility, which Kitty and I enjoyed only last summer. I found it quite interesting that the middle daughter, Marianne, who is but sixteen falls in love with a handsome cad named Willoughby. I guess it was because I'd written down my thoughts on Wickham that I was struck how similar in nature these two men were. Also, the fact their surnames begin with the letter 'W'.

This story cheered my heart somewhat as Miss Marianne Dashwood did find love with Colonel Brandon, a quiet man who was quite a few years older than she. This gives me hope for us, Maxwell. Twelve years is not too much time. Why, Admiral Pennyroyal is almost twenty years his wife's age and they adore one another.

Have I told you how grateful I am, that it was you who rescued me that night at the inn? When he, (I refuse to call him by any name), snatched me from my bedroom and carried me off to that horrible inn, I prayed as never before. I shudder to think what would have befallen me if you hadn't heard my cries.

Your brother, Nathan, stopped by for a brief visit. He was quite curious as to why you were in London, and as I didn't have the faintest idea for the reason of your absence, other than business or Parliament, I couldn't provide an answer. I must beg your forgiveness. During our brief conversation, I told him about your letter and he asked to read it. He became quite perturbed and spoke briefly with Mr. Chapman and Mrs. Howell. Soon after that, he returned home. He said I'd done nothing wrong, but I'd shared your private correspondence and I'm sure he was disgusted by my behavior.

I'll finish my ramblings with more antics from Sir Waddlesworth. He has returned to the house. Your stable master begged me to take him back as he howls all night and puts the horses on edge. Poor Sir Waddlesworth. I suppose he missed my soft, inviting bed because he snuggled near my feet all of last night. I am glad of his return as well and appreciate his company in the music room as I work on my newest music. I do hope you will enjoy my latest attempts when you return to Adborough Hall.

I miss you and I love you,

Georgiana Kerr

Max stared at the waning fire in the fireplace, the letter held loosely in his hand. This missive explained why Nathan had barged so unceremoniously into Kerr house a few months back. It made him wonder, given how he'd treated Georgiana, why Nathan hadn't planted a facer on him for his boorish behavior. Truly, before the Lord got a hold of his youngest brother, he not only would have punted Max a good one on the nose, but would have laid a well-deserved beating on the rest of him.

Nathan's angry words pummeled his memory.

You've treated her worse than a harlot. You have subjected her to an embarrassing scrutiny for reasons she has no knowledge of.

Max tipped back his head and closed his eyes at the painful memory. How right Nathan had been and how wrong he'd been. He truly was the worst libertine of them all. She was an innocent maiden and he'd become judge, jury and executioner of their marriage without a fair trial. Georgiana would hate him when she learned the truth.

He carefully folded the letter and placed it with the others before locking them in his desk. He didn't think his heart could take any more, not after her latest revelation of never having been intimate with a man. There was only one more letter to read and no others had been delivered these past few weeks. That did not portend well for him.

Chapter Fourteen

Max handed his outer clothing to Benson before moving down the hall to his study. The strident tone of his mother caused him to pause mid-step.

"Maxwell Edward Phillip Kerr, stop right there."

It was a rare day when his mother called him by his full name and he was loath to turn around, much like his ten-year-old self would have been, and yet he did. Mother stood framed in the door of the front drawing room, back rigid, hands clasped tightly in front of her. He didn't know if that was because she was trying not to shake or was holding herself back from throttling him. Instantly he knew Nathan had spoken with their mother about his estrangement with Georgiana.

"Yes, Mother?"

"I will have a private word with you." She looked toward Benson. "Ensure that his Grace and I are not disturbed. For any reason."

"Yes, your Grace." Benson bowed and removed himself from the hall, taking Max's outwear to the cloak room and then disappeared through the servant's door.

"To your study, Maxwell. The room is fairly soundproof with all the books lining the wall and I can be assured of a modicum of privacy there."

With a regal swish of her skirts, his mother moved past him and down the hall to his study. He followed behind and closed the door when they reached his inner sanctum. Still holding herself straight and tall, she turned and faced him, tears flowing down her face.

Shocked, he quickly approached and held her in his arms, letting her cry silently against his chest. After a few minutes, she clenched her hand into a fist and gave his vest a few hard pounds before stepping back. Silently, he handed her a handkerchief, which she used to dry her eyes. When she finally looked up at him, the anguish in her gaze nearly brought him to his knees. He'd never disappointed his parents, nor given them any cause for grief, and yet he'd brought his mother to tears.

"There are no words to describe how angry I am at you. When Nathan informed me of your callous disregard for that lovely girl I jumped to your defense. My first impulse was to come back to Town and ring a peal over your head, but Caroline was so close to delivering Margaret—"

"They had a girl?"

Max fell into the closest chair. Nathan had not been kidding when he said he was cutting Max out of their lives. He hadn't even informed him of the birth of their first child.

"Yes. Nathan forbade me from writing you with the news. As soon as Caroline was comfortable with my granddaughter, I returned to deal with this mess. George offered to escort me, but Catherine is nearing her confinement and he's reluctant to leave her side. Nathan said he'd never darken your door until you apologized."

"George and Catherine are expecting a child as well?"

"Maxwell, I am at a loss over your behavior. Not only have you treated Georgiana with callous disregard, but both your brothers refuse to speak your name. It's as though you've died a traitor's death."

"I may well have. All of this is my own doing."

"Then explain it to me. The only way forward is to take that first step." She settled in a comfortable chair by the fireplace and looked at him expectantly.

He stayed seated for a few minutes, gathering his thought and then stood to pace. As he walked back and forth in front of his desk, he haltingly told her of what all had transpired.

"...when I heard Darcy say he couldn't make this one go away, I thought my heart would stop. What did he mean by this one? I was immediately reminded of the incident with Lady Celeste and my imagination fell into a deep well. I've never been taken over by rage before and I let it consume me in the foulest manner."

"You never spoke to Darcy, or even to Georgiana?"

"No and I regret to say I began to look upon her abduction by Slade in a different light. Had she been willing and only cried out when he became too rough with her? She was only in her nightgown and no one knows how long they were in the room together—"

"Enough! No wonder your life is in shambles. You have known this young woman for almost her whole life. If you think for one moment she would agree to an assignation or hasty marriage to Sir Reginald Slade, then you belong in Bedlam. Anyone with an eye to see knew she loved you. She lit up when you came into the room and although I can't verify this, I believe she's loved you for a long time, maybe even longer than you have loved her."

"That would be impossible."

"And now we come to the crux of the problem. Answer this question honestly, Maxwell. Have you ever spoken to Georgiana of your true heart, or did you assume everything would fall into place once you were married? Does she even know your fears and why you did this absolutely stupid thing?"

"I've never told her about Celeste and her treachery."

"Surely you gave her some inclination as to why you were leaving so soon after your wedding?"

"I…" He thought back to the letter he wrote before leaving Adborough Hall, where he told her she could be in no doubt as to why he was going back to London, alone. How could she know? The whole two days it took them to reach his estate he'd not spoken more than a dozen words to her, and none of them respectful. He treated the scullery maid with more esteem.

He fell into the chair again and dropped his head into his hands.

"I thought not."

"I have since learned she is quite innocent of any machinations I imagined and am at a loss at how to proceed. I have wronged her grievously, Mother. There may be no turning back."

"No, there is no turning back." She stood and smoothed down the front of her skirt. "You created a fine mess and for once I am not going to lend you aid. I must take my leave as I promised George we would leave for his estate when our interview ended."

"George is here? I thought you said he wouldn't leave Catherine's side."

"He also didn't want me traveling alone."

"Is he in the other parlor?"

"No, he chose to wait in the stables. Like your brother, he has no desire to engage you in any way until you've made apologies. All of us are displeased with you, Maxwell. This is NOT how I raised my sons to treat their wives, let alone any woman of any standing. Do not bother to see me out."

With that, she exited the room and he heard her call to Benson to bring her cloak and advise George she was ready to leave. He sat in contemplative silence before he sat behind his desk and brought out Georgiana's last letter, noting that his hand shook.

October 27, 1814

My darling Maxwell,

This will be the last 'letter' I write as my journal has arrived and I now have a lovely leather-bound book in which to jot down my dreams and wishes. In some ways I will miss writing you. Penning my thoughts in this format has allowed me some time to heal and fill the lonely hours. The rest of my time is taken up with keeping Sir Waddlesworth out of the cook's domain. He is determined to find every scrap of meat she drops.

Mr. Mason and I visited the tenants again to check on those to which I'd taken some needed food stores

I cannot finish this as my brother has arrived and I depart this night for Pemberley. I am now fully aware of what you think and my heart is truly broken. Anna is packing my trunks as I write, so I must sign off and tuck this letter away until I have returned to Pemberley. I know not how I can go forward. I am such a fool and can only find comfort in the fact no one else knows of my stupidity.

Max dropped his head into his hands and groaned. He was the fool, not Georgiana. How could he, for even one minute, have believed her as being a woman of loose morals? He did not deserve her love and once she reached Pemberley, he knew Elizabeth and Fitzwilliam would take her in hand and advise her to annul the marriage.

His heart constricted and a physical pain shot through his chest. He couldn't lose her, but he also couldn't storm up to Pemberley and demand his wife be returned to him. Legally, he could, but if he wished to have a wife and a normal marriage, he had to make amends. And make amends fast.

Even though he'd not heard from Adborough Hall, he knew – without a shadow of doubt – his wife was innocent of all the treacherous things he'd despaired over. He reached for his stationery and dipped a new quill into the inkpot.

My darling wife, Georgiana,
May I call you Georgiana, for that is how I think of you...

As he sanded, then folded the letter to be sent, sinking his signet ring into the soft wax, he felt a burden lift from his shoulders. There may be no turning back, but he would create a new trail. One that held only him and his love. He had to trust God to make straight his crooked path.

~~~~~

"A letter for you, my Lady."

Georgiana took the letter from Anna and felt her whole body grow cold when she recognized the seal. The formal address on the letter mocked her.

Her Grace, the Duchess of Adborough
Pemberley, Derbyshire

Maxwell!

As though burned, she dropped the letter on top of the pianoforte where she'd been playing a difficult piece in an attempt to empty her mind of thoughts of her husband and a life that might have been.

How did he know she was at Pemberley? Her insides began to shake. He'd been explicit that she was not to leave Adborough Hall without his consent. Did this missive contain words of anger and a demand for annulment? She pushed away from the pianoforte and moved toward the Paladion window overlooking the back garden. A light snow covered the ground, creating an illusion of peace and tranquility. She touched her brow against the cool pane of the window. If only her thoughts mirrored the pastoral scene before her.

She glanced over her shoulder at the letter, laying on the pianoforte, mocking her with its fake title. Had he sneered and toyed with more thoughts of her doing evil when he was forced to write down her legal name? It would not have given him joy, that was for sure.

"Have you finished playing, Georgiana?" Lizzy entered the room at a slow pace. She was only a few weeks from delivering and Fitzwilliam had given strict orders she was to limit her time on her feet.

"Yes, I cannot concentrate on Handel today."

Lizzy noticed the letter on the pianoforte. She glanced at the address and her eyebrows rose a fraction higher.

"From his Grace?"

She nodded, not daring to speak lest she blurt out something in anger, and she was trying very hard not to be angry any more. The emotion drained her and he wasn't worth the effort anymore.

"Well, at least he didn't address it to the whore of Babylon."

"Lizzy!" Her sister's black humor made her smile, but only a little. "I don't think he thinks of me as the whore of Babylon, only of Derbyshire."

Lizzy laughed out loud. "Well done, Georgiana. I knew you had a stiff Darcy spine. It's high time you came out of your doldrums and start a new chapter."

"I suppose I should read what he has to say." She picked up the letter and sat down beside Lizzy.

"You do not need to do anything." Lizzy laid a hand on hers. "You can consign it to the fire without opening it, much like Fitz does with any correspondence from Lady Catherine."

Georgiana turned the letter over in her hand and toyed with the edge of the sealed fold. Warring thoughts chased through her mind. Read it. Burn it. Read it. Burn it.

"I need to see what he has written." Decision made; she broke the seal. His first words clawed at her heart and she forgot to breathe.

My darling wife, Georgiana,
May I call you Georgiana, for that is how I think of you.

Almost verbatim, he'd copied her form of addressing him in her private letters. How could that be? She finally took in air and looked up at Lizzy, who demanded. "What? What has he said?"

"He called me his darling wife."

"He what?"

"I need to speak with Anna."

"Your maid? For whatever reason?"

"I have no time to explain, I shall return in but a moment."

She hurried from the room and asked one of the footmen to direct Anna to her suite of rooms. Within a few minutes, Anna appeared and after a quick curtsy, asked, "What can I do for you, my Lady?"

Georgiana stopped her pacing.

"Do you recall me asking if you'd taken care of my letters prior to us leaving Adborough Hall?"

"Yes, ma'am, I do. I wrapped them up in a pink ribbon so that they wouldn't get separated."

"And what, exactly, did you do with them?"

"I gave them to Mr. Chapman to post to his Grace in London." Anna paused and began to wring her hands. "Did they not make it to his Grace? I was so careful with them. I'm sorry, my Lady—"

"You did nothing wrong." She broke into her maid's apology. "I was not specific enough in *my* direction to you." She sat at her desk, letter in hand. "Thank you, Anna. Please tell Mrs. Darcy that I will see her at dinner."

"Yes, my Lady." Anna curtsied and backed out the door.

What to do now? Max knew everything. How she felt. Her confession about Wickham. All her secrets and fears. Her soul had been laid bare and she had nothing to lose. She looked at the letter in her hand and began to read.

Chapter Fifteen

Georgiana sat gazing out her bedroom window, the letter held loose in her hand. Her mind whirled in frantic circles. What to do? Write back or ignore Maxwell completely as he had done her the past four months? What course of action should she pursue? None left her feeling satisfied, or content.

The clock struck the hour and she realized she'd been in the same attitude for over two hours. At almost the same time her stomach rumbled and she remembered she'd not eaten since breaking her fast that morning.

She tugged the bell pull, summoning her maid and tucked the letter in the top drawer of her desk. Within minutes Anna entered and she began to dress for dinner. While Anna fixed her wayward curls, Georgiana made up her mind to ask Lizzy for advice. Her sister by love had never led her down a wrong path and this decision was too momentous to make on her own. She didn't even entertain the thought of asking her brother. Fitz would not be able to see past his own anger and she desperately needed the level-headedness Lizzy demonstrated on a daily basis.

Once dressed, she took the letter, folded it into a smaller rectangle and slid it into one of her hidden side pockets. Lizzy and Fitz had not come downstairs yet, so to occupy her time and mind she picked up the blanket she's been stitching for one of Pemberley's tenants and waited for their arrival. She'd completed one small pattern by the time they made an appearance. Unexpectedly nervous, she set aside her stitching and stood.

"Do you mind if we proceed to the dining room right away, Brother. I have not eaten since breaking my fast this morning and my stomach has kept up a steady conversation with me for the past half hour."

"As you wish, Georgiana."

Fitz signalled Carson to notify the kitchen, then offered his arm to Lizzy and the three of them made their way to the family dining room. This was one of Georgiana's favorite rooms. It held only a smallish table, seating up to eight with ease, two sideboards and wide comfortable chairs that made one want to linger at the table. In the morning, the room was bathed with sunlight and in the evening, the moon cast its warm glow over the gardens which beckoned beyond the terrace doors.

"Lizzy tells me you received a letter from his Grace," Fitz murmured between the first and second course. She should have known her sister by love would not keep such momentous news secret and yet she experienced a twinge of disappointment. She wished to discuss the letter with Lizzy alone, although... Fitz *had* been more than conciliatory in his dealings with her over the past few weeks and he deserved to know what Maxwell proposed.

"I have and he has given me leave to share what he wrote with you and Elizabeth."

"He gives you leave−"

"Fitzwilliam, you promised to remain calm."

Lizzy laid a restraining hand on her husband's arm and he abruptly closed his mouth into a thin, disapproving line. Georgiana had seen that look upon his face only once. The day he turned Wickham out of their rented house in Ramsgate.

Georgiana reached into her pocket and pulled out the letter, passing it over to Fitzwilliam.

"Elizabeth, would you read it first. I'm afraid I may not hold my temper in check and will trust you'll share the salient points." Darcy signaled the footman to leave and asked they not be disturbed for the next half hour, whereupon the dessert course would be served.

After the footman had departed and fully closed the door, Lizzy opened the letter and began to read silently.

"No, this will not do. I must know what he wrote." Fitz bit out between stiff lips. "Please read it aloud, Lizzy."

"Very well," she answered and complied.

My darling wife, Georgiana,

Fitzwilliam snorted and Lizzy raised an elegant eyebrow at him.

"Sorry my love. I shall behave."

She smiled softly and continued reading.

May I call you Georgiana, for that is how I think of you. I am in *receipt of your letters. All five of them and have no hope of others being delivered any time soon. I want to, nay, I <u>need</u> to say:*

I am a complete and utter ass.

"We all know that," her brother muttered.

"Fitzwilliam Darcy. If you interrupt one more time, I shall discontinue reading and not share any of what Maxwell wrote until tomorrow evening."

"You wouldn't."

"Don't try my patience. I'm heavy with child. I have a toddler who demands all my time and energy throughout the day and I haven't slept properly in over a month." She shook out the letter in agitation. "Shall I continue?"

"Yes, my love. I will remain as quiet as a church mouse."

"Pfffttt....," was Lizzy's only reply before beginning again.

I have no explanation for my words and actions other than an incident which occurred in my youth and, if you return to Adborough Hall, I shall share the full of it. Know this. I betrayed not only your trust but my good judgement. How could I have entertained such vile thoughts about you? There is no plausible answer or reasoning other than the fact I became consumed by jealousy. I broke not only the trust of your family, but mine. You are a gracious and lovely young woman not deserving of my previous bitter treatment. My mistakes are multiple and egregious.

Fitz snorted and Lizzy gave him a warning twitch with her eyebrow. He clamped his mouth tight and leaned back in his chair. Georgiana dreaded the next part of the letter, unsure of how her brother would react.

I am well aware that words without action are hollow and with that in mind, I beseech your permission to attend Pemberley and work through this trying time. Have no fear of me demanding your return to Adborough Hall. I solemnly promise I will never dictate your actions again and your family may stay by your side as we converse. I desire there be no secrets between any of us. To that end, I have no objection to your sharing this letter with your family members.

The information I overheard with regard to Wickham was something we should have spoken of prior to our wedding. However, looking back, I realize there was no time. Between social engagements, fittings for your trousseau and all the excitement that goes along with organizing a wedding we had no time for ourselves. One does not have this conversation on the edges of a ballroom, nor at a musicale. I believe you would have told me. It's not your nature to be dishonest. I've always known that. I allowed jealousy to color my view of your character.

Although I never spoke the words aloud, I proclaim them now. I love you, my darling Georgiana, most ardently. I have loved none but you.

I await your reply,

Eternally yours,
Maxwell Kerr

"He can wait until Hades has frozen over. That man is not welcome at Pemberley."

Fitz pushed back his chair and threw his napkin onto his

plate. Lizzy let him stew for a few minutes before speaking.

"I seem to recall a certain gentleman who also made multiple mistakes in his pursuit of love. He almost lost the woman he so ardently loved because of extreme prejudices against her family and interfered with her sister in an extremely high-handed way." She paused and gave Fitz a compelling look. "Need I go on?"

"There is no comparison between the two incidents," he groused. "Adborough insinuated that Georgiana dallied with not one, but two different men." Fitz sat once again and drummed his fingers on the table.

Georgiana paled at the vehemence in her brother's voice. If she did reconcile with Maxwell, there remained a good possibility she'd lose her brother forever. The choice was almost too difficult to consider.

"And whose fault might that be?" Lizzy argued back. "I don't wish to point fingers at you, or Richard, but surely to goodness one of you should have informed him of Wickham prior to their marching down the aisle. Nathan told us Max was completely blindsided by the news and, yes, he behaved badly, but he did it out of a jealous love. And we all know what a twisted partnership love and jealousy make."

"I reformed my character upon your chastisement—"

"Please, stop!" Georgiana stood, her whole body shaking. "I cannot stand the fact you are debating over who behaved more badly. I have the beginning of a headache and wish to return to my room." She held out her hand and Lizzy gave her back the letter. "I shall see you both in the morning."

With that she spun on her heel and exited the room, almost at a run.

~~~~~~

A soft knock on the door had Georgiana pause in her pacing.

"Georgie?" Her brother's muffled voice carried through the thick door.

She moved to the door and swung it wide, not waiting to see if he entered before moving to sit in the chair by her fireplace. Fitz took only a few steps into the room and played with his signet ring. Determined not to begin the conversation, she waited.

"I have no words for my callous disregard for your feelings in this matter."

She refused to interrupt him, even though she could tell he expected her to voice an opinion.

"Elizabeth kindly reminded me that you are a married woman, and as such, I must have what she called an adult conversation with you. Something I don't believe we've ever truly had."

"No, we have not."

Fitz sat across from her and leaned forward, placing his elbows on his knees. He looked... forlorn, and her heart strings tugged.

"You were only ten years old when Father died and I went from loving older brother to guardian and father figure in one short minute. At twenty-two years of age, what did I know of raising a young girl, or of running an estate? My answer was to place you in a safe school and when it became apparent you weren't thriving in that environment, I sought to pack you off with a governess or companion. It's my fault Mrs. Younge had the means to perpetrate her fraud with Wickham. I did not practice due diligence in checking her background."

"You did the best you could, Brother."

"Did I?" he countered. "Could I not have spared my younger sister a few short weeks of my company while I awaited a response from Mrs. Younge's 'so-called' references? What was happening in my life that I could not spend those days with my one and only sibling? Were you not worth the time and effort?"

"Cease this crazy talk." She stood and wrung her hands with agitation. "I know you love me and I know you did the best you could."

He also stood and took her hands in his, stilling their movement.

"I do love you, but I did not do my best by you. In all things important, I behaved as badly as Maxwell. Maybe even worse, because I have known your character far longer than him."

"Oh, Fitzwilliam," she threw herself into his arms. "I don't know what to do."

"As much as it pains me, you must write back to Adborough. I leave it up to you whether or not you wish him to attend Pemberley. Elizabeth and I support you no matter what your decision may be. You will always have a home with us."

She leaned back in his arms and cupped his cheek with her palm.

"You have always been the best of brothers and I will sleep on my decision and let you know on the morrow." He turned his face and kissed her palm before she stepped out of his loose embrace. "If I know Lizzy, she awaits your return so you may tell her all is well between us."

"You know her well, Poppet."

"You've not called me that in years!"

"And I probably won't ever again. You are no longer a child in pigtails and pinafores." He paused in the doorway. "Sleep well, Georgiana."

"I'll try," she whispered as the door closed with a soft snick.

Sleep eluded her as thoughts of Maxwell and his letter, of his behavior and apology circled in a continuous loop. It was only when strings of pink and orange streaked across the eastern horizon did the haze of Morpheus relax her mind. Before breaking her fast later that day she picked up her quill, dipped it into a new bottle of ink and began writing.

~~~~~

"The post has arrived, your Grace."

Benson placed a pile of correspondence on the corner of Max's desk. Before his butler had closed the door, Max pawed through the letters, stopping only when he recognized Georgiana's handwriting on one of them. The week awaiting her reply had been excruciating. His whole attitude had been one of half hope and half agony. Everything rode of her decision.

With shaking hands, he broke the seal and began reading.

Pemberley, Derbyshire
November 14, 1814

My Lord Duke,

I am in receipt of your letter dated November 8. After carefully consideration, I have requested and received permission for you to attend Pemberley at your earliest convenience. My brother awaits your response in order to have rooms prepared in advance.

In good conscience I cannot have you arrive without advising that my cousins, the Viscount Ashton and Colonel Fitzwilliam will also be in attendance. They are set to arrive sometime next week and will remain at Pemberley through to Twelfth Night.

On a personal note, I beg you destroy the letters I wrote. My maid mistakenly mailed them, not realizing they were for my own particular use.

Regards, etc.,
Georgiana Darcy Kerr
Duchess of Adborough

Max read the letter several times, saddened by how stilted and formal she sounded. Even though he understood her embarrassment and desire for the letters to be consigned to the fire, he could not comply. Not when the pages were filled with how much she loved him. He treasured every word written and they'd have to pry them from his dead, cold fingers.

He checked his calendar and decided to leave in two days. The prospect of a quiet, personal visit had diminished upon Georgiana's revelation that her two cousins would be in attendance. She was amassing a formidable army that would protect her by any means at their disposal. However, he counted on the blessed fact that she had loved him as his best weapon to breach her defenses. He'd make sure Clarkson brought extra shirts and cravats for him. Knowing the Fitzwilliam brothers' temperaments, he expected double trouble in the form of fisticuffs and words. It was best to be prepared for the worst, although he prayed for the best.

~~~~~

Max opened the well-worn Bible he'd pulled from his valise. He'd gone into the library to spend a few minutes of quiet before leaving for Pemberley. A heavy sigh lifted his shoulders and with his hand resting on his most treasured possession, other than his wife, he released his breath, letting frustration and worry expel alongside.

"Lord, have I lost everything? My lack of trust in Georgiana unforgiveable. Guide my thoughts and words as I go forward rebuilding my marriage." He glanced down at the Bible, opened to the book of Joshua. "I need the fortitude and faith of Joshua to slay the giant of my pride."

He closed in eyes in contemplative silence, opening them only when the door crashed open. Viscount Ashton burst into the room; anger etched deep in his face.

"Your Grace, I apologize. I explained to the Viscount you were not receiving." His butler, clearly distraught, followed Ashton into the room.

"It's all right, Benson. You may go."

With a polite bow, Benson left the room, closing the door behind him. Not sure what Ash would say or do, but willing to receive a verbal chastisement, Max stood. He moved so fast Max barely had time to blink before Ashton had his throat clutched in a deadly grip. Gasping for breath, he struggled to break free from the larger man's strangle hold.

"You may have wrestled with younger brothers, your Grace," Ash leaned close to his face and growled, his breath hot on Max's cheek, "but Darcy, Richard and I grew up with Wickham."

For the first time in Max's life ice cold fear crept through his veins and snaked around his heart. The venomous hatred in Ashton's voice, as well as the unspoken truth that anything learned from George Wickham was underhanded and foul, cautioned him to tread lightly. He tried, unsuccessfully, to twist out from Ashton's hold.

"You abandoned my cousin" – the fingers squeezed again – "sentencing her to solitary confinement without so much as telling the prisoner her supposed crime. Darcy is too much of a gentleman to attack you physically. Richard would run you through with his sword, but as a Colonel in his Majesty's military he'd face court martial and deportment, if not the death sentence. I, on the other hand, have no plans of ever marrying and carrying on the Matlock name. It would be my honor to make Georgiana a widow."

"Ash," Max choked out and patted the Viscount's arm in the unspoken way of surrendering to a more capable opponent. "I love Georgiana."

"You love her!"

"Yes."

With a bitter laugh, Ashton released his grip and stepped back. Max coughed as much-needed air made its way into his lungs. With a sound of disgust, Ashton turned to leave. When he reached the door, he turned abruptly and faced Max.

"You are a hypocrite and a fraud. A deceiver of the worst kind." His voice vibrated with anger. "You may love your horse, or your newest vest, but you do not love my cousin."

"I do love her," Max reiterated and straightened to his full height, his bruised pride smarting over the idea that Ash believed he loved only inanimate objects. "My recent behavior is unacceptable" – the Viscount snorted indelicately – "however, if Georgiana chooses to look beyond this and forgive, I ask that you follow her lead. All I can do is prove my words with action."

"There is a story in the Bible where the Lord caused the sun to stand still. You need a miracle of that magnitude to earn back my cousin's trust. To earn back ALL our trust."

For the first time in months he felt the stirrings of a smile. He knew nothing was impossible with God.

"You and I both know that if the Lord can make the sun and moon stand still, He can soften the heart of the sweetest woman ever created. I will do my part and the Almighty will do His."

"If you plan to stand on prayer alone, you'd better ask Him to give Elizabeth a heart full of forgiveness. *She* is the one you should fear, not Darcy."

Max knew Elizabeth Darcy was a formidable woman in her own right, on par with his much beloved mother. Diminutive in stature, her intelligence and strength of will was the stuff of legend. If she chose to oppose a reconciliation between himself and Georgiana, his task would become exceedingly difficult.

"I'm well aware this task, without Divine intervention, is nigh unto impossible."

Ash reached for the door handle and then paused.

"Adborough," he said, without turning around. "It's been

a long time since I thought God held any interest in the affairs of man. If you manage to earn back the love and respect of our family and friends, I may have to revisit my long-held doubts."

"Then it's imperative that I succeed."

The Viscount half turned and held Max's gaze. "I almost hope you do."

Chapter Sixteen

Brittle leaves covered the walkway which lined the edge of a lake near the front of Pemberley. Georgiana and Lizzy, arm in arm enjoyed a slow walk along its path. Given the advance state of Lizzy's condition, this was the only place Fitz allowed Lizzy to take her daily constitution because, although close to her time, she refused to stay abed.

"Have you given any more thought of the Duke's intentions to attend Pemberley?" Lizzy queried between short breaths.

"I have thought of nothing else since Fitz received his letter."

They came to a stop and Lizzy placed one hand against her side and grimaced.

"This child is moving so much I can barely catch my breath."

"We are almost at the bench Fitz installed for you. Give me your arm and we'll rest for a bit before going back into the house."

With a soft thank you, Lizzy took Georgiana's arm, placing much of her weight against it and they moved at a snail's pace towards a bench. Without warning, Lizzy stumbled and even though Georgiana held tight to her arm to soften the fall, she dropped heavily to her knees.

"Lizzy!" Georgiana cried out and helped her move into a sitting position, uncaring if both their skirts became embedded with mud and snow. "Oh, dear Lizzy. Are you all right?"

"No… Ooooooo." Elizabeth sucked in a sharp breath and clutched her belly. "Not now, not now, not now…" she whispered and drew in another deep breath.

"What must I do? Can you stand?" Georgiana looked around to see if anyone had noticed them from the house, but she and her sister were obscured from sight by a clump of coniferous trees.

"The child is coming, Georgiana." Lizzy bit her lip and closed her eyes. "Find Mrs. Reynolds and have her send for the midwife and also a few footmen to carry me to the house."

"I cannot leave you alone—"

"We have no time for this." Lizzy's voice brooked no argument. "I twisted my ankle and am unable move on my own. You have no choice."

"I shall see if I can find Fitzwilliam—"

"He has gone with his steward to assess one of the tenant's cottages. He will not get back in time."

Georgiana gripped Lizzy's elbow and tried to help her stand. Lizzy moaned softly and before Georgiana could move, a large hand reached between them. Surprised, she glanced up and saw Maxwell leaning over them, his face grim. Where had he come from? She hadn't heard a carriage, or horses.

"Lend me your hand, Mrs. Darcy. I shall carry you to the house."

"I'm far too heavy for you to carry."

"Nonsense." In deft, efficient moves he gathered her up and cradled her effortlessly in his arms. Lizzy wrapped hers around his neck and shoulders. "You are still as light as a feather."

"Careful with your words, your Grace. I know I'm a heavy load to carry over treacherous ground."

"I said light as a feather, Mrs. Darcy. I didn't specify which bird."

Lizzy started to laugh and then caught her bottom lip between her teeth, another moan escaping in place.

"If you intend to take me indoors before this child makes an entrance, I suggest we move now."

"As you wish."

Max began covering the ground with sure strides. Before he reached the front steps, the door opened and Mrs. Reynolds hurried out to greet them, two footmen following close behind.

"Oh, Mrs. Darcy. What happened?"

"Mrs. Darcy requires a doctor, or midwife, if that is the arrangement she's made." Max answered for Lizzy who'd begun to pant from the contractions.

Mrs. Reynolds stopped and gaped at Maxwell, torn between anger at his treatment of her girl, Miss Darcy and admiration that he was taking care of her beloved mistress.

"The midwife is but a few miles from here, I'll have a footman bring her right away."

"And have Stephens send out a rider for my brother,"

Georgiana ordered, finally rousing herself from the shock of seeing Max. "Fitzwilliam will want to be advised as soon as possible."

"Right away Miss Darcy – forgive me – your Grace." Although a furious blush colored Mrs. Reynolds cheek at her faux pas she quickly directed one of the footmen to carry out the orders before facing Maxwell again. "Creighton here can carry Mrs. Darcy to her room, your Grace."

"There is no need Mrs. Reynolds. I do not see the need to give her any more discomfort than what she already has. If you would lead the way, I shall follow."

"Yes, sir." Mrs. Reynolds paused and caught Georgiana's eye. "Would you care to attend Mrs. Darcy now or wait until she's settled?"

"I'll wait until she's settled. I need to find Anna and have her bring up the supplies we've prepared for this moment. Also, I need to advise Lizzy's physician. I'm sure he would like to be here in case there are any difficulties, not that Mrs. Andrews is not a competent midwife."

"Very well." With a brisk nod of approval, Mrs. Reynolds turned to Max. "If you would come this way, your Grace."

Max spared Georgiana a quick glance and smiled ever so slightly before ascending the staircase with his precious load. Loathe to go upstairs too soon and run into him before getting her thoughts in order, she handed her outerwear to a waiting maid and quietly asked her to find Anna and begin preparations. By this time, their butler had appeared and she gave instructions for the doctor to be called out.

"Before I send a footman with the note, would you like some tea. I'm sure it will help settle your nerves before the big event."

"Carson, you are a life saver. Can you have it brought to the breakfast room?"

"Yes, your Grace."

She hurried to the breakfast room and sat facing the window. A light snow had begun to fall, coating the bare trees with a soft blanket of white. The pastoral scene outside was calm and peaceful, yet her mind whirled with worry. Lizzy wasn't due to deliver the baby for at least two to three weeks. She prayed quietly the fall hadn't hurt the child and that both mother and babe would be healthy. Her thoughts then turned to Maxwell. His arrival, though not unexpected, was also premature. While grateful he'd arrived when he did, for Lizzy's sake, what precipitated his early arrival?

The door to the room creaked open and she turned expecting one of the staff members to enter with her tea. Instead, the large frame of her husband filled the doorway. She rose to her feet and faced him properly for the first time in nearly five months.

"Good afternoon, your Grace," she finally managed to say.

"And to you, Georgiana." He accompanied his greeting with a small nod. "I hope you don't mind that I joined you. Carson indicated he was bringing tea, and I have to admit, I'm parched."

"No, I don't mind, your Grace. I shall leave you to it while I attend my sister."

She started toward the door but Maxwell did not move aside. Unsure of what to do, she paused.

"Georgiana, please don't rush off on my account. I know you are angry, with just cause. I have come, heart in hand, to beg your forgiveness and begin to make amends for my past behavior. Can you please stay for but a few minutes before seeing to Mrs. Darcy?"

"You ask for a few minutes to forgive your foibles when you could not spare any time to even introduce me to your staff?" She drew herself up to her full height, which was considerable given her family genes. "My sister's baby will not wait for anyone, not even a Duke, and I will attend her. Please stand aside. Now."

Max moved to his right and she swept by, head held high.

~~~~~

Max closed his eyes and drank in the light scent of honeysuckle which lingered after his irate wife made her way upstairs. He'd known he would not be welcomed to Pemberley and as such, had prepared himself for barbs and subtle insults. What he hadn't anticipated was the cold depth of Georgiana's anger.

"What did you think? That she'd open her arms wide and tell you how much she loved you?" he muttered.

"You finally figured it out." The droll tone of Ash gave him a start. The Viscount strolled by, clipping his shoulder with his own as he entered the room exclaiming, "Splendid. Carson provided tea."

Max shoved down his disappointment and followed Ashton into the room. A footman hurried to provide both of them with a cup of tea and then, very discreetly, left the room.

"Have you been here long?" Max asked, not really caring for an answer but wished to dispel the heavy silence. He thought he detected fatigue around the eyes of his former friend, but Ash led such a dissolute life it very well could be world weariness.

"We have only just arrived. In fact, given the state of your horses at the carriage, I'd say we were about an hour behind you."

"You didn't leave him alone—" Colonel Fitzwilliam burst into the room, stopping short at the sight of Max. Instant anger tightened the Colonel's lips into a thin line and he began stalking toward Max, who'd risen to his feet. Ash stepped in front of his brother and stayed his progress with a steady hand against his chest.

"Let me at him, Edmund," Richard growled.

"Keep a cool head, brother. I spied Georgiana heading to the second level and our dissolute Duke was here, alone, in the breakfast room. We were about to have tea. Care to join us?"

"I'd rather eat my own boots."

"Normally I'd say, 'have at her', but this is a perfect time for us all to sit down and have a conversation."

"Who says I want to speak to that prat?"

"Because this was the whole purpose of why I came to Pemberley," Max said before resuming his seat. "Have you seen Darcy?"

"Afraid of coming face to face with her brother?" Richard sneered.

"Not in the least."

Worried, but not afraid. There was a vast difference in attitude.

"How do you explain the reason you're still in your traveling clothes?"

"I haven't had time to change. We sent rider out for him

because Mrs. Darcy is in labor—"

"Why didn't you say that in the first place!"

Richard swiveled and exited the room, shouting orders to bring his horse around to the front of the house. Ashton glanced at Max and assessed him.

"You couldn't have led with that when I came into the room?'

"What, and take away your joy of digging the knife in further?"

"There is that," Ash conceded with a wry smile.

"Your brother also interrupted before I had a chance." Max blew out a soft sigh. "I arrived and spotted both Georgiana and Mrs. Darcy walking along the lake's edge. I then saw Mrs. Darcy fall, quite hard, and immediately went to give aid."

"Is Elizabeth well? The baby?"

"As far as I could ascertain, and I'm no physician, she hurt her ankle and was unable to walk, plus she went into the early stages of childbirth."

"How did she get back to the house?"

"I carried her."

"You!" Ash exclaimed in obvious disbelief.

"Yes." Max ground out between clenched teeth. "Me."

"Hmmph… Good job, Adborough. There might be some redemption in this for you after all."

"Thank you so much for your glowing approval," Max said with a touch of cynicism.

"Tuck that sarcastic tongue back into your mouth, your Grace. Do not forget you are persona non grata within this house. You hurt a most beloved member of our family and we Fitzwilliam's and Darcy's have long memories."

"I'm well aware. Georgiana did not even spare me a greeting, although that was to be expected given her concern for Mrs. Darcy."

"The fact you were there in their time of trouble may soften the edges of their anger, Adborough. If you're truly repentant, and I suspect you are, it will show."

"Ashton, I never know when you're being sincere or yanking my chain. However, I'm taking your words at face value because that's all I have right now."

Max stood and with a stiff bow toward the Viscount exited the room and made his way to his suite of rooms. Prior to his despicable behavior toward Georgiana, he'd always enjoyed his stays at Pemberley. This time, the bright room did not dispel his heavy spirit. While his valet, Clarkson, continued to unpack his trunks, he sat in the chair by the window and prayed.

He prayed for Elizabeth and Darcy's baby and for Georgiana. Even if their marriage ended before it truly began, he didn't want her to go through life bearing a deep grudge. He wanted her to be happy and was willing to let go if she demanded it of him.

The next few hours were tense. Darcy arrived hard on the heels of the midwife, followed closely by his physician. Although he knew he wasn't entirely welcome, Max forced himself to join the family as they waited in the drawing room.

Georgiana remained cloistered with Elizabeth and her male relatives prowled restlessly around the room, tossing disdainful looks and remarks toward him. He drew deep upon the words of his father of how to face great hardship. Remain calm and hold your tongue. If you do not provide a raging fire fuel, eventually it will die out. Give your adversaries time to cool off.

After a few hours of dour looks, Mrs. Reynolds came into the room and told them Mrs. Darcy was faring well. Relief flooded through Maxwell and he quietly thanked God for answered prayers.

"Mrs. Reynolds. Please thank the footmen who brought my wife into the house."

"It was his Grace who helped Mrs. Darcy. He carried her up to her room and made sure everything was taken care of."

Darcy shot a look of surprise at his brother-in-law and exchanged a few quiet words with his trusted housekeeper. Shortly after Mrs. Reynolds left, he approached Max.

"Thank you," Darcy said in a low voice.

"I was there at the right time and did what any gentleman would do given the circumstances."

"Regardless. You made sure my wife was taken care of in a most expeditious manner."

"Do not disregard your own sister. She kept her head about her and made sure you were summoned."

"I'm glad we agree about my sister on something. Once again, thank you." Darcy gave him a half bow and returned to his cousin's side. Ashton raised a brow and his brandy glass toward Max. Richard grunted and continued to ignore him.

"Mr. Darcy."

Carson slipped through the door and approached his employer, whispering a few words into his ear.

"Have Mrs. Reynolds prepare their rooms for them and the children."

"Right away, sir." Carson left the room and the door closed softly behind him.

"What is it, Darce?" Richard asked.

"Bingley and Jane have arrived. I sent an express as soon as I could. I know Lizzy will want her sister with her at this time."

The door to the drawing room opened again and this time the nanny entered with a tousled hair toddler in her arms.

"I'm sorry, Mr. Darcy but Master Bennet refused to go to bed until he'd seen his Papa."

Darcy held his arms wide and the nanny passed the little boy over to his father.

"What's wrong, my boy. Have you missed your Papa?"

The child, who had the dark curls of his mother and the blue eyes of his father nodded his head before popping his thumb into his mouth.

"Where Mama?" he lisped around his finger.

"Mama is busy having a baby and tomorrow morning you will be a big brother."

Master Bennet removed his thumb and cast a disdainful look at his father.

"I am not a bruver. I am a Darcy."

Ash and Richard both chuckled and Max couldn't help but smile at the determined set of Bennet's jaw. Even at his tender age he was a replica of his sire, right down to attitude.

Darcy cast an apologetic look at his cousins and began walking toward the door. Evidently, he planned on escorting his own child to the nursery and settle him down for the night. Max had a sudden vision of carrying his own child through the halls of Adborough Hall. If he hadn't bungled his own marriage, he and Georgiana could have been expecting their own child at this very moment.

He remembered how Elizabeth's light body had tightened in his arms with each contraction. Never before had he realized how much a woman went through to bring forth children and he set a mental reminder to thank his mother most profusely the next time he saw her. That was, if he saw her again. Unless he made amends with Georgiana, his family could well disown him for life. His future looked exceedingly bleak and he experienced a sudden, keen sense of loss.

"Are you well, Adborough?" Viscount Ashton took a step toward him. "You've gone quite pale."

"I'm fine." Max fumbled for his pocket watch. "I have had a long day and believe I'll retire for the night."

He exited the room and before the door closed completely, he heard the two brothers speaking.

"Come now Richard. He's trying to make amends."

All Max heard in response was a low grumble from the Colonel.

"When you've lived a completely honest and virtuous life, then and only then can you sit in judgement of another. Cast not the first stone, brother."

Max couldn't stop the smile that lifted the corner of his lip at Ash's defense of his character, but what made him almost laugh was Richard's response, which resonated through the closing door.

"Have you been reading your Bible?"

Chapter Seventeen

"Jane, I am so glad you've come."

Georgiana rushed toward her sister-in-law and gave her a hard hug. The past few hours had been fraught with tension, starting with Lizzy's fall, sending her into premature labor and ending with the knowledge that her husband could very well be stalking the halls, waiting for her to exit her sister's suite of rooms.

"Fortunately, we had decided to come early in case of bad roads and were already packed to leave on the morrow. Although it's only thirty miles, I don't travel well when I need to make frequent stops."

"How are you faring?"

Jane and Charles were expecting their second child early in the new year.

"Other than the fact I can no longer see my toes and rely on my maid for matching shoes, I am hale and hearty." She shrugged off her shawl and accepted a work apron from Anna. "Is Lizzy in the other room?"

"Yes. The midwife and physician are with her."

Jane started toward the connecting door before she paused and faced Georgiana, taking her hands in hers.

"How have *you* been faring? This is a new and terrifying experience, I'm sure." Jane's soothing voice acted like a balm on her soul.

"I'm holding up remarkable well, seeing as I am not the one trying to bring a babe into the world." She gave Jane's fingers a squeeze before releasing them. "Thank you for asking."

"You are stronger than you know." Her blue eyes caught and held Georgiana's. "When you finally have a conversation with him, try to remember he is a man who made a mistake. I cannot believe the Duke, who has such a caring heart, would behave in such a manner without good cause. Not that you gave him good cause," she quickly added at Georgiana's gasp. "I meant in the manner that *he* believed he had good cause."

"I heard your sister once said to you that she could forgive my brother's pride if he hadn't injured hers."

"Yes, she did." Jane laughed softly at the memory.

"Max didn't just injure my pride. He believed me capable of a most heinous deceit. He tore out my heart."

"Oh, Georgiana." Jane gathered her into another tight hug. "Men in love do the most ridiculous things. And he does love you. Of that I have no doubt. Before you and the Duke married, he could not keep his gaze off you. Trust me when I say that you are *his* heart and I'm sure he regrets his past actions." She released Georgiana and stepped back. "I must attend Lizzy, but know that you are in my prayers."

"I'm sorry for keeping you from your sister."

"Do not apologize. I'm sure Lizzy will not mind I spared you a few minutes. You know she would say the same thing."

A short, hard laugh erupted from Georgiana.

"I don't think my sister-by-love is as kind as you. She would expect me to make him grovel."

"That is where you are wrong." Jane shook her head slowly. "Lizzy has decided opinions to be sure, but when it comes to the heart, she's as much a romantic as me. Even when she was livid with Fitzwilliam, she always despaired over his inherent goodness. She didn't want to reconcile the dichotomy of his character, yet we are all glad that she did."

"You've given me much to think on, but all of this is conjecture until I actually speak with his Grace."

"I would have that conversation sooner rather than later." Jane moved toward the door and paused, her fingers on the door handle. "As evidenced by today's emergency, none of us know what tomorrow holds."

She pushed down on the handle and entered the room.

"Jane, you are here!"

~~~~~~

Georgiana took her time getting dressed before heading downstairs to join her family, and Max, for dinner. As she descended the staircase, she envisioned Max dressed as a common laborer. It was something Lizzy told her to do when she became flustered and needed to regain her equilibrium. However, upon entering the drawing room all thoughts of Maxwell dressed as a laborer fled from her mind as soon as she laid eyes on him.

Even though they were not dressed formally as dinner was

a light repast being served in the family dining room, Max was still so handsome in his every day clothing he stole her breath away. She forced herself to give him only a cursory glance and focused instead on the other occupants within the room. Charles Bingley broke the ice by surging forward and giving her a brotherly hug.

"Georgiana, it is so good to see you again. Did you get a chance to speak with Jane before she attended Elizabeth?"

"I did." She took Bingley's proffered arm and glided toward her brother and cousins. When her fingers trembled ever so slightly, he covered them with his own warm hand. "Lizzy will be so glad she has arrived. There are times when you need family close at hand."

"Can I get you something to drink, Georgiana?" Fitz asked when she reached his side.

"Not at this time." She needed to keep her head clear in order to deal with Max.

"Georgiana."

She gave a start at the sound of Max's voice and turned to find him standing only a few feet away. He gave her a polite half bow.

"May I have a few words with you before we partake in dinner?"

She hesitated briefly, loathe to leave the comparative safety of her sibling and glaring cousins. Or rather her glaring cousin. Singular. Richard wore a dark look, Ashton seemed pleased.

"You may," she replied with a slight nod.

He offered his arm, but she ignored the gesture and moved past him toward a grouping of chairs on the other side of the room. She settled in a comfortable chair and waited as he took the seat opposite her.

"I must first apologize for treating you in such a repulsive manner. I have no excuse except a deep-seated jealousy and a bitter reminder of an incident from my past, which drove me to believe the absolute worst. Not once did you, in any way, behave in a manner that justified my actions."

"The polite thing would be to thank you for your apology, which I do. However, your actions showed me, in no uncertain terms, that you have absolutely no regard for my feelings. I wonder if you ever did. I even wonder if you truly loved me."

"I do love you, and have done so for a very long time."

"Really? Pray tell me how? What drew your attention to me? I am not yet twenty."

Max sighed heavily and rubbed his fingers over his brow. Finally, he glanced up and held her gaze.

"I once told Nathan I was drawn to you because you did not see the world through rose colored glass. Instinctively, I knew you had experienced deep sorrow and grown from it and when you finally fell in love, it would be deep and abiding. I desperately wanted to be the man who received your affection."

"You did have my affection, and my love. You were also my everything and I had loved you for almost as long as you say you've loved me, but that does not excuse your behavior." His heart and hope sank at the reference to her love in the past tense. "I cannot trust you to betray me again if things don't go the way you plan. My heart cannot take another blow. I'd rather be alone for the rest of my life and forego my own children than take the risk." She stood and Max rushed to his feet as well. "Our discussion is finished, your Grace."

She gathered her skirts and joined Fitz and her cousins. When Carson announced dinner was ready, Fitz held out his arm to her and escorted her into the informal dining room.

~~~~~

In spite of his hurt and frustration, Maxwell couldn't help but be proud of the way Georgiana comported herself. Beneath all that velvety softness lay a core of tempered steel. He should have seen that before. His wife was no wilting flower, only a shy one. She was a Darcy, through and through.

He shook his head and followed everyone into the breakfast room. His rank should have given him precedence leading into the meal, but after everything which had transpired over the past few months, he was grateful to be allowed at the table. Among these people he was not the Duke of Adborough, but the man who broke Georgiana's heart. A humbling experience, indeed.

Darcy seated Georgiana to his right and Ashton quickly took the remaining seat beside her and Bingley next to Ash. Richard took the chair to Darcy's left, which forced Max to either sit at the end of the table by himself or beside the prickly Colonel. He decided to engage the bear and slid in beside Richard, although he kept a wary eye on the man's flatware, in case he decided to spear him with a butter knife.

The first few minutes, spent with gathering food and footmen bustling about filling water pitchers and pouring tea, gave way to a heavy silence which fell over the room like a funeral pall. The scrape of cutlery on fine china began to grate on his nerves and he debated whether he should try and start a conversation, if only to keep from hearing himself chew food. Finally, Darcy broke the silence by addressing Bingley.

"How did Jane fare on the trip here. She is so close to her own confinement I wondered if she'd come at all."

"Jane was splendid, as always. It was Henry who chafed at being confined in the carriage. Mrs. Preston had her hands full keeping him occupied."

"How old is the little chap?" Ashton asked.

"He celebrates his first birthday on Christmas Eve."

The door creaked open and Darcy's heap whipped 'round to see who entered, hope and worry evident on his face. Carson came and whispered in his ear.

"Thank you, Carson." Darcy dropped his napkin onto his plate and surged to his feet. "Excuse me, but I must go and attend my new son."

"Oh, brother! That is good news," Georgiana cried out. "And how is Lizzy?"

Darcy turned at the door and grinned so wide Max almost didn't believe this was the same stoic man he'd attended University with. "She is well. Very well indeed."

Immediately following Darcy's exit, Georgiana briefly touched her mouth with her own napkin before standing. Immediately, all the men stood with her.

"Excuse me, but I must attend my sister as well."

Before Max could utter a word, or offer to escort her upstairs, she'd exited the room, leaving him with the Fitzwilliam brothers.

"Isn't that marvelous," Bingley mused to no one in particular. "Darcy will be proud as a peacock, I dare say."

"How is Caroline and the baby, Bingley?" Max carefully

broached the subject of his brother's wife, unsure of how much Bingley knew of why there was such an undercurrent of hostility.

Although he arched an eyebrow toward Max, he answered affably, "She and Margaret are thriving. Louisa came and stayed with her during the confinement and delivery and Jane and I spent a few days with them after. Lord Nathan is well pleased with his family." Bingley flushed slightly and fumbled in his speech. "His immediate family…. That is his family at Moreland Manor."

"Bingley." Max bit back a sigh. "There's no need to dance around the fact my brother is not speaking with me."

"Nathan has cut you off?" Richard exclaimed.

"All my family has, as you well know."

"I didn't know, but it warms the cockles of my heart to hear that." Richard slapped his thigh and barked out a hard laugh. "How does it feel to be on the outs? No one to have conversation with. Not that anyone cares. You must have countless hours on your hands to spend in self-examination, ruminating on what a prat you are."

"Trust me, I have examined my actions. They were deplorable."

"Right you are there, your Grace," Richard sneered, leaning into him at the table. "Tell me, because Darcy is as tight-lipped as a monastic monk, what set you off about Georgiana? What did that poor girl do to deserve your derision?"

"I don't think this is the place to discuss my reasons." Max shot a worried look toward Bingley. He had no idea if he, or Ashton knew of Georgiana's experience with Slade and

Wickham.

"We're amongst family. There are no secrets here, right gentleman?" Richard cast a glance around the table.

Bingley fidgeted and Ashton gave his brother a warning glance, but the Colonel was in high dudgeon and he'd obviously been chomping at the bit to have a piece of his hide. Max considered his words carefully before answering.

"I overheard a conversation between you and Darcy after the wedding breakfast." He watched the Colonel's face to see if he remembered what their conversation had entailed. The Colonel's expression remained void of any emotion. "Darcy said he could not make this one go away."

Understanding flashed across Richard's face and he abruptly sat back in his chair.

"Are you speaking about Miss Darcy's... I mean, her Grace's previous experience at Ramsgate?" Bingley said and everyone gaped at him. He offered them an awkward smile. "There are no secrets between my wife and her sister either, although this has not gone beyond Jane and I."

"*He* may not have knowledge, you dolt!" Richard hissed at Bingley, tilting his head toward Max.

"I do know of Wickham," Max replied with a calmness he clearly did not feel.

"What? How?"

"Georgiana told me herself, well not tell me exactly. It was in a letter she'd written."

"To you. A letter written to you." Richard's tone indicated he did not believe his cousin would have written him about anything.

"At the time I believed they were written to me as they

were posted to my house in London and had my name on them. Every letter was addressed to me."

Richard opened and closed his mouth several times before sending his brother a quick glance.

"You said, 'at the time'. What exactly did you mean by that?" Ash took the reins of the conversation from his brother.

"I have since found out these letters were for her own specific use and that she'd had no intention of me ever receiving, let alone reading them."

"Did you return them?"

"I have not." Before anyone could speak another word, he added, "And I will not."

"But, you must! How else do you expect to earn her trust again?" Ash exclaimed and threw his napkin onto his plate.

"She doesn't want his trust," Richard also threw his napkin down and stood. "I demand you give me those letters and I shall return them personally to my cousin."

"They are the only words I have of her telling me she loves me and I will not give them up."

Max rose to his feet, his appetite completely gone. With a perfunctory half bow, he pivoted from the table and exited the room, a swish of silk his only warning that Georgiana had been in the hall and heard everything he'd said.

Chapter Eighteen

"They are the only words I have of her telling me she loves me, and I will not give them up."

With her heart beating a frantic tattoo and Max's heated words ringing in her ears, Georgiana backed away from the door and hastened down the hall. Did he truly love her? If yes, then his declarations of felicity and admiration had a ring of truth and she could no longer believe he was only trying to trick her into returning to Adborough Hall so his sterling reputation would remain intact before society.

How could she trust him? For years he'd been so conciliatory and kind and then overnight believed the very worst of her. What if she displeased him again? Steady footsteps sounded behind her and she desperately wished she could break into a run. She wouldn't be in this predicament if she'd not forgotten her fan in her haste to leave with Fitz and avoid sitting at the table with her husband.

"Georgiana," Max called quietly.

That he didn't wish to call attention to the fact she'd

eavesdropped on their conversation, unwillingly, lessened her anxiety somewhat. She halted her steps and waited for him to come alongside.

"May I walk with you?" he asked.

She nodded and they walked toward the music room at a more sedate pace. Not a word passed either of their lips, yet the silence did not become oppressive. He waited for her to enter the room, then followed. After a brief hesitation he turned back and shut the doors.

"Fear not," he said with a rueful smile. "I only wish for a modicum of privacy before your cousins begin to seek us out and save you."

Against her will, her mouth tilted into a small smile.

"They have become my champions."

"And rightly so."

He moved toward a couple of elegant chairs near the pianoforte and, with a small flourish of his hand, invited her to sit down. He took the chair opposite and turned his attention to window, watching snow fall gently to the ground. Unwilling to break the amiable silence, she gazed intently at his profile.

She took note how his jacket seemed looser about his shoulders and chest. He'd lost weight since she'd last seen him. She was no better. Her maid lamented daily how she no longer fit her dresses and had been taking them in for months. If they kept this up, they'd become known as the skeletal Duke and Duchess of Adborough. She gave an inelegant huff at the thought. He turned at the sound and caught her looking at him. Blushing furiously, she dropped her gaze.

"Something amuses you, Georgiana?"

"It is nothing," she started to say, then changed her mind.

"A passing thought caught my fancy."

"Would you care to share this passing fancy?"

She assessed him, not sure how to take this light form of conversation after so many heated words between them. A wave of longing washed over her. *This* was how their marriage should have been right from the start. Throwing caution to the wind, she replied, "You and I have not fared well in this whole escapade."

"How so?" His expression became one of wary surprise.

"Am I right in thinking you have not been sleeping well?" He nodded slowly. "Food has no taste or texture and you eat to maintain your health and nothing else?" Again, he nodded in response. "And you wonder how people find any joy in their life?"

"Yes. Has it been the same with you?"

"Yes, your Grace."

"Stop saying that!"

"Saying what?"

"Your Grace. How I hate the sound of those two words from your lips." He rose and moved to the fireplace, staring into the flames. "I regret, wholeheartedly ever ordering you to address me as such."

"Maxwell..." He turned to face her; eager hope etched on his features at her calling him by name. "What are we going to do?"

"I'd like to start again. Wipe our slates clean, as it were." He returned to his chair and leaned forward until his forearms rested on his thighs, his whole demeanor entreating her to consider his idea. "I'd like to court you, Miss Darcy."

Her eyes widened in response to him calling her by her

former name.

"You'd like to court me?"

"Yes, and the first thing you need is a chaperone."

He stood and moved to the bell pull and summoned a servant. In less than a minute, Carson opened the door and bowed slightly.

"Could you please summon Miss Darcy's maid to attend us please."

The usually unflappable butler reacted with a raised eyebrow at his mistress being addressed as Miss Darcy but he rallied quickly and said, with a polite half bow. "Right away, your Grace."

"Maxwell, this is ridiculous." She rose to her feet and began to pace. "You cannot court your wife. It's unheard of."

"This makes perfect sense. Of course, I shall have to improvise, being that we are not in London, but I shall court you, Miss Darcy and hopefully win your heart and hand."

A dread thought chilled her to the bone.

"If you are not successful in this endeavor?"

"Then, I will grant you an annulment," he said in a quiet voice and her heart dropped into the pit of her stomach.

It was then she knew. She wanted him to succeed. No, she needed him to succeed. She desperately wanted to love him again, without regret and without boundaries. He could not fail or her heart would splinter into a million pieces.

Pemberley
March 1815

Georgiana raised her face to the sun, its weak rays piercing through the clouds and glass enclosure of the orangery after a cold winter. Ever since her brother had seen the Prince Regent's orangery at Carlton House in 1811, he'd worked hard to create a luxurious place to grow their own exotic fruits and vegetables all year round. She'd retreated there for some privacy in order to re-read Max's latest letter, however, excited giggles reminded her the glass enclosed structure was also a favorite haunt of her nephews.

She rose and folded the missive, hiding it in one of the pockets sewn into her dress. She didn't have to wait long before two nannies, pushing Fitz and Lizzy's first-born Bennet and his cousin, Henry Bingley turned the corner.

"Down!" Bennet cried out upon seeing her. "I want Auntie G."

Nanny lifted Bennet out of the pram and set him on the pebbled walkway. Georgiana crouched down and allowed the stout toddler to run into her open arms. Henry wasted no time in joining his cousin in a warm hug.

"Well, you have found me. Now I'm curious as to why when you know I shall see you later when we have nuncheon."

"No nunchin," Bennet pouted. "Want that."

He pointed his chubby finger toward the bare apple tree beside them. She lifted her nephew and brought him closer to the tree.

"Do you see any apples, Bennet?" She wondered if he even knew what an apple looked like given that he was only five months past his first year and smiled when he reluctantly shook his head. "That is why you will want a snack later on. Eating a tree will not fill this belly."

At the word belly, she tickled his tummy. He giggled and

wriggled in delight until Henry tugged at her skirt.

"Me too," he cried out.

Georgiana set down Bennet and quickly tickled Henry and for a few minutes enjoyed the innocent wonder of her two nephews. If she hadn't had such a disastrous start to her marriage, she might have been awaiting a child at this very moment. What she wouldn't give to hold her own son or daughter in her arms, but was that longing enough of a reason to forgive Maxwell.

"Who's ready for a glass of milk and some biscuits?" she asked when they'd settled down.

"I am," both boys said in unison.

"Then, go with Nanny and wash your hands. I shall join you shortly." She signalled the nannies to take charge of the boys and once they'd exited the orangery, sat on a nearby bench and retrieved her letter. A soft, furry body joined her and she lovingly scratched him between the ears.

Adborough Hall
February 26, 1815

My darling Georgiana

I sit and look out the window watching what is hopefully the last winter storm of the season. With the advent of spring my soul is hopeful of new beginnings. Not only with the season and Parliament, but with our relationship. I received your letter and devoured it within minutes of Chapman placing it upon my desk. I am pleased your new 'guest' arrived safely. It took much coaxing for Mr. Mason and I to bring Sir Waddlesworth out of his hiding place and into a comfortable box for transport. The scratches received will be heralded as badges of honor if he brings you joy.

As before, I will share what I love about you. We've covered the first seven letters of the alphabet, bringing us to the letter 'H' and for me, that means your heart.

I love your heart.

You fascinate and inspire me and because of you, I strive to do better. My heart is full of you. There are no others in my thoughts, which consume me day and night. Every night, before I go to bed, I gaze at the stars, comforted by the thought that you could be looking up at those same celestial orbs with me. A tenuous bond, at best, but one to which I will cling because it brings me closer to you.

I love you, my darling Georgiana.

Yours, etc.,
Max

P.S.

I leave for London for the start of Parliament next week. My dearest hope is that you, and your family come down for part of the Social Season. I desire to escort you to the theater and, if I may be so bold as to ask now, may I have the first set of any ball of your choice.

~~~~~

"What am I to do? He loves me."

Georgiana had joined Lizzy after she'd settled Andrew for his nap.

"Are you sure his love is constant and not a desire to present a united front to the world." Lizzy poured a cup a tea and handed it to her. "He is an important man and must produce an heir. You are his only option. I know not how to counsel you in this matter, Georgiana."

"His letters have not wavered in his declarations of devotion. He…" she hesitated in sharing what Max had written but her sister-by-love never quibbled with giving her opinion and she needed somewhat of an outside voice to see reason. "He has begun, alphabetically, cataloguing all the ways he loves me."

"He has?"

"Yes. First there was alluring, followed by beauty, compassion, devotion, ethereal, felicity, my own name and finally, my heart."

There was a brief moment of silence until Lizzy broke it by saying, "Oh dear, what will he do for 'x'?"

They both began to laugh and Georgiana felt some of her trepidation depart.

"You and Fitzwilliam both had strong prejudices against one another when you first met. How did you overcome those obstacles?"

"As you well know, when your brother sets his course, he rarely deviates from it. He had determined to become a better man, or to be more precise, a man whom I could respect without reservation. And so, he persevered while I remained unaware of his steadfast love until Lydia's folly with Wickham. If she hadn't blurted out how he had discovered them, I may have never known of his deep regard for my wellbeing." Lizzy set down her tea cup. "If you truly love him, Georgiana and wish to have, at the very least a comfortable life with him, then I believe you need to take the first step. He said he will not impose without your permission. It is now up to you."

~~~~~

It had been two weeks since he'd sent the letter to Georgiana, with no reply. Had he lost her for good? Could he keep his promise to grant her an annulment if unsuccessful in reclaiming her love? All he wanted was for her to be happy, and if that meant he had no place in her life, then he would have to accept her decision.

Tears pooled in his eyes and his heart clenched. The pain was physical and he dreaded facing every moment she was no longer his. Despondent, knowing he only had himself to blame, Max returned home after a long day in the House of Lords.

The butler met him at the door and divested him of his hat and gloves.

"The mail has arrived, your Grace."

"Thank you, Benson. Advise cook that I'm ready for my dinner."

He'd started toward the family dining room when Benson spoke again.

"It is incumbent upon me to advise that a particular letter awaits you, sir."

"A particular letter?"

"Yes, sir. In a pale cream envelope tied with a pink ribbon."

"Thank you." He couldn't help the flutter of hope burgeoning in his chest. "Please tell cook to hold supper for a few more minutes."

"As you wish, sir."

He gave no thought to the enigmatic smile his faithful butler bestowed upon him as he quickly strode toward his study and his desk where the letter awaited. His hands trembled as he slit the envelope open and began to read.

Kerr House
April 1815

    My Indelible Maxwell,

    The next letter of love is 'I' and as an equal partner in this relationship, I claim the right to share my point of view. First, I find you Intriguing and Impassioned in your quest to restore our relationship and, for me, you are Incomparable to any other man I know. Second, I am Impatient to begin a proper courtship and await you in the music room.

    Yours, etc.,
    Georgiana 'Darcy'

She was here! The letter and ribbon fluttered to the floor, forgotten in his haste to barrel out of the study toward the music room. Sounds of Mozart danced upon the air and when he opened the door all of his attention was riveted on the one he loved more than life itself, seated at the pianoforte. Silent, not wanting to break the spell of her artistry, he drank in her beauty.

She glanced up, and not missing a beat, smiled. When the piece was complete, she stood and moved away from the instrument and began to walk toward him. Without thought, he met her halfway until they stood but a few feet apart.

"You have come."

"Yes, it is time for us to begin again."

Uncertain of how exactly to do that, he clasped his hands behind his back and rocked a bit on his heels. He suddenly felt like a young swain standing in front of an irate father, wishing to ask if he could dance with his daughter. Of the two of them, Georgiana seemed the most composed, but then she'd been planning this visit and he was still galloping madly along, trying to catch up. From the corner of his eye he caught sight of Mrs. Annesley, Georgiana's companion from before her marriage. He turned and gave her a slight nod.

"Mrs. Annesley. How very good to see you."

He almost flushed at the slight lie. He *was* glad, yet not glad she was there. He wanted none other than Georgiana, yet these were the very parameters he'd set in place before he left Pemberley in December.

Be careful what you wish for, for that is what you will receive.

"You as well, your Grace," she replied with a deep curtsy.

"Mrs. Annesley has agreed to come on as my companion during our courtship. I hope you do not mind?"

"Not at all, I think it is a brilliant idea. Would you like some tea?" he asked, finally remembering his manners.

"We must decline as Aunt Matlock is desirous to meet Fitzwilliam and Elizabeth's newest addition to the family regardless of the hour. I promised to return and spend time with my family."

He wanted to shout, '*I am also your family*', but wisely kept his counsel. Mrs. Annesley gave him a small nod of approval, as though she'd read his thoughts. He turned and escorted them to the front door where Benson awaited.

"I have an invitation from Fitzwilliam to give you and your mother." She brought a card out of her reticule and handed it to him. Without looking, he palmed the card in his hand.

Georgiana fussed with her gloves and a slight blush colored her cheeks and he had a flashback to the young girl she was before all this nonsense began. Maybe the young lady he'd fallen in love with, and who had loved him back was not lost, only hiding behind blankets of disappointment and hurt. A barrier he longed to peel back one layer at a time.

"Tell your brother and his wife that I will happily attend." Before she could turn and exit, he whispered soft enough so only she could hear, "I love you still, my darling Georgiana."

Her gaze flew to his and he became lost in the cool depth of her azure eyes. Too soon, she smiled slightly and lowered her gaze.

"Good day, your Grace."

And she was gone.

He'd almost reached the study when her words finally impacted on his brain and he fished out the invitation only to find there were two. One to him, the other to his mother.

"Benson!"

His butler appeared within seconds of his calling out.

"Your Grace?"

"Miss Darcy has left an invitation for my mother to dine at Darcy House. Has the Duchess given any indication she will be here for the occasion?"

"Your mother has not said anything to me, sir, however, she may have mentioned something to Miss Darcy when they had tea this afternoon."

"Tea?" His head spun. "Here? This afternoon?"

"Yes, sir. The Duchess is resting in her chambers and advises she will see you at dinner. She also requested to forego changing this evening as she wishes to have an informal night with family."

"Family," Max struggled to wrap his thoughts around everything Benson relayed. "And how many will be attending this informal, family dinner?"

"By all accounts, your Grace, six adults including you and your Mother, and two infants. Her Grace enlisted the aid of the housekeeper to prepare the nursery for the children and their nannies."

Slightly dazed by the overload of information, Max thanked Benson and returned to his study. Everyone, his mother, his brothers, their wives, their children, were coming to dine with him tonight. He sank into a chair by the fireplace and allowed tears to flow down his cheeks while he thanked God for bringing his family back into his life.

~~~~~

"I knew I'd find you here."

At the sound of his brother's voice, Max looked up from his ledgers to find George at the door to his study. Uncaring if it was indecorous or not, he stood and almost ran to his brother, enveloping him in a tight, bear-like hug upon reaching him. George returned the hug and then slapped him on the back before stepping away.

"I was unsure if you would welcome us back into your home, brother. It's been a long time, nearly seven months." George said with his usual good humor.

"You and the rest of the family have been on my mind continuously. I could only hope and pray you would forgive my behavior and begin anew." Max replied, thankful his voice didn't crack with emotion.

"Mother requires our presence in the drawing room before dinner."

Another familiar voice beckoned from the doorway.

"Nathan!" Max moved to his youngest brother and enveloped him in a hug as well. "I am so glad to see you."

"And I, you."

"I must tell you that you were right."

"I was?"

"Yes, when you visited me all those months ago. You were right to lay down the gauntlet of truth at my doorstep, so to speak." Keeping his arm around his brother's shoulders, Max turned to face George. "He wisely advised me to take the beam out of my eye before I judged another."

"Our youngest brother has become a fount of good advice. I've looked to him for good cheer and warm words these past few months as I struggled with some decisions for Catherine and I."

A shaft of disappointment stole his breath at the stark reminder of how far his family had moved from him. His closest brother had not thought to seek his counsel, something which he had done with absolute trust until this debacle. His pride had cost him more than a happy marriage and he could only hope the fraternal bonds were strong enough to overcome everything.

"Shall we join Mother, before she sends Benson to gather us up?" he asked, dropping his arm from around Nathan's shoulders.

"Maxwell." George stepped forward and held his gaze. "Much has been said and acted upon this year that we all regret.

You made a mistake, but through the correspondence between Catherine and Georgiana, and" – he cast a quick glance toward Nathan, who nodded – "and Caroline, we know you are making amends and seek forgiveness. And we do forgive you, whole-heartedly."

"That is truth," Nathan offered, "but we'll cut you off at the knees if you ever do something like this again."

Max's gaze flew to Nathan's and even though his brother smiled, there was steely determination in his eyes.

"Well then," he tugged at his vest and smoothed it down. "for the sake of my cobbler I shall make every attempt to never be a nod-cock again."

The brothers moved in unison toward the drawing room where their mother awaited. When she rose to her feet and met Maxwell half way, and allowed him to wrap his arms around her, he knew his family was on their way to reconciliation. All that remained was reclaiming his heart. Without Georgiana, any portion of his life was empty and dull.

Chapter Nineteen

"His Grace, the Duke of Adborough."

The butler announced Max's arrival and he, along with his mother, entered the drawing room to complete silence. For a brief moment he hesitated until his mother pressed her fingers into his forearm and he remembered to move forward. His discomfort was alleviated somewhat by Elizabeth leaving her husband's side to approach them both, a welcome smile upon her face.

"Your Grace," she curtsied before them both and mother released his arm to break protocol and take Elizabeth's hand in hers.

"We are so pleased you invited us to join the family for dinner."

"Thank you, your Grace—"

"I insist you call me Margaret. We are no strangers here."

While Elizabeth and his mother chatted, he cast his attention about the room, locating Georgiana on the far side, conversing with Catherine. Caroline, seated on the other side of Georgiana, rose to her feet and approached him.

"Maxwell," she took his arm and led him over to Colonel Fitzwilliam. "I have it on good authority that the good Colonel claims to have beaten you and George in a three-legged race when you were all young lads. My husband, who partnered him, has no recollection of this epic affair."

Max shifted with unease. He was unprepared to face Georgiana's cousin so soon into the evening. He thought he'd have at least an hour before the situation presented itself. Obviously, Caroline was not one to beat about the bush and decided to bring things out into the open.

"I know we had many such games when we were young lads running about the estate, but I do not recall any specifics."

"Unlike you, your Grace," the way Richard drawled the words 'your Grace' made them sound like an insult, "I have an excellent memory. It is unlikely I will forget anything that has happened between the two of us."

"Stop it, Richard." Both men looked at Caroline in shock. "Your false bravado does no good here and we are commanded to forgive. I suggest you have a long talk with my husband, followed by extensive reading of the book of John."

A dull hint of red tinged Richard's neck above his cravat. He mumbled something unintelligible and moved away.

"That was lovely." She moved the two of them in the direction of a glowering Darcy. "Shall we beard the lion in his den?"

He desperately wanted to say 'no', but his sister-in-law, with a surprisingly firm grip, steered him across the room. They stopped directly in front of the Darcy's and his mother.

"Mr. Darcy, Elizabeth, Mother Kerr." Caroline said,

smiling at all of them. "My husband and I have decided the best way to facilitate this unusual family reunion was to allow all parties to converse and begin healing. If we remain tight-lipped in our polite corners, nothing will change and Georgiana will become distressed."

Caroline kept her arm looped through his, effectively pinning him in place. He couldn't be sure, but he thought Elizabeth's eyes danced with humor. His mother turned her head to one side and he saw that, she too, was trying to hide a slight smile.

"Adborough," Darcy offered with a polite nod of his head.

"Darcy," Max returned the greeting.

The silence stretched between them. This was worse than when they were at Pemberley. He decided to take the first step.

"I thank you for extending this invitation to dinner."

"The invitation came from my sister."

Undaunted, Max continued, "Regardless, you had the option to not attend, yet here you are."

"Yes, here we are," his mother said. "And it's time to be a family." She turned to Elizabeth. "Tell me more about your new baby. I'm dying to know how he fares after such an abrupt entry into this world."

As his mother and Elizabeth conversed about Andrew, Max assessed Darcy. He knew that his friend's good opinion once lost, was nigh unto impossible to regain, and yet he had to try for Georgiana's sake. He cast a glance across the room and noticed that although she still conversed with Catherine, she kept careful watch on him and her brother. He offered her a slight smile to quell any concerns she may have had and she returned it swiftly.

"She was very nervous about this evening," Darcy offered in a soft voice. "I haven't the heart to disabuse her of the notion that we can attain our former friendship."

"Why disabuse her at all. We may not go back in time, but we can proceed forward. Our friendship has changed, that is a fact, but I have always held you in high esteem and nothing has changed my attitude toward you. I regard you as a friend and hold out hope that someday you might reciprocate."

"Someday, Adborough, but not today. Can we agree on that?"

In spite of himself, Max found himself smiling. "We can agree on that."

"Elizabeth has told me how, multiple times, how grateful she is for your timely arrival when she'd fallen at Pemberley."

"Truly, Darcy, 'twas nothing. It was God's providence that I arrived when I did and could help in any way."

"Regardless. She said you were most solicitous and then she commented on something you said while carrying her into the house."

"Really? I wonder what that could be."

"She wondered to which bird you referred."

His brow furrowed as he cast his mind back to when he'd carried Elizabeth into the house. At the time he'd been so worried he murmured a few kind words so that she wouldn't panic and possibly hurt the child. At last, his memory lit on a part of the conversation to which Darcy alluded and chuckled.

"I take from your reaction that you have recalled your words."

"I do," Max cut a quick glance toward Mrs. Darcy who had paused in her conversation with his mother. "I made reference to an ostrich."

Elizabeth arched an eyebrow and said with a smile, "An ostrich?"

"Yes, Mrs. Darcy. A very large ostrich."

Elizabeth laughed outright before clapping a hand over her mouth.

"You have won this war of words, your Grace. I shall gracefully concede before you decide to enumerate how many feathers it would take to replace my body weight." She looked toward his mother. "Later, when the gentlemen have their port, I'll share more details."

"I look forward to it," mother replied with a curious glint in her eye. "And then, I'll tell you some stories about your husband and his cousins that will make your toes curl."

"You must tell me everything. I'm dying to know what they were like as children as they refuse to tell tales about each other."

"It's called righteous blackmail, my dear."

Max took this opportunity to excuse himself from their company and made his way to Georgiana. He knew every eye in the room followed his progress.

"Georgiana." He gave her a polite nod once he arrived where she waited.

"Maxwell."

A somewhat awkward pause began before he remembered his manners and addressed Catherine. "Did you find the confectioner's store Mother told you about?"

"I did and spent over an hour browsing. The shop was filled with so many delightful things I couldn't decide what I wanted to purchase."

"I have it on great authority," Maxwell leaned toward the two ladies as though imparting a great secret, "Your husband is a regular customer there."

"That is no secret, Max. I recognized the store's logo as soon as I saw one of the gift boxes."

"Nathan spoke of this shop." Caroline had joined them and stood by his side. "Right next to the haberdashery he frequents, if I'm not mistaken."

Max used this opportunity to come closer to Georgiana.

"Would you take a turn about the room with me?"

"I would be delighted."

She stood and looped her arm through his before they began to amble about the edges of the room.

"I received your letter this morning," he murmured, nodding a polite hello to Elizabeth's sister Mary. She was seated between Colonel Fitzwilliam and his brother, Ash. "I'm not sure kind is a word I would have used in our little adventure through the alphabet."

"Of course it is. Other than your aberration last year, you have been nothing but kind."

"Thank you, Georgiana. The next letter is mine and I decided I would tell you personally, rather than in writing." He took satisfaction in seeing her cheeks pinken ever so slightly. "The letter 'L' has me dreaming of love, and I'm filled with longing for your lilting laughter."

"Pffftt…" was all she said, yet her eyes twinkled with humor.

"You find me too loquacious with my lyrical prose?"

They'd stopped in front of the French doors, slightly opened to let in the warm night air.

"It's my turn," she replied. "The letter 'M' has me thinking of your name. Maxwell."

"That's only one of my names."

"Do not interrupt."

"Yes, my lady."

"What are you two whispering about?"

She abruptly stopped speaking as Ash joined them. Maxwell cussed beneath his breath and the sideways glance Georgiana slid in his direction told him she'd heard. The corner of her mouth quirked when he gave his shoulders a slight shrug before facing the Viscount.

"The alphabet."

"The what?"

"We are talking about the alphabet and the importance of its letters."

Ash swiveled his gaze between the two of them, clearly unsure if Max was yanking his chain or telling the truth.

"It's quite true, cousin. We have been extolling the virtues of the alphabet and have reached the letter 'N'. Care you to join us?"

"No, as in 'N', 'O'."

"Delightful. We have now reached the letter 'P'. Maxwell, what say you?"

"Perfection. Everything about you is perfection."

The smile she gave him glittered. Yes, she was perfection and he wanted more than anything to whisk her through the open doors onto the terrace and kiss her perfectly plump lips, but Hutchins appeared at the door and announced dinner was ready to be served. Max extended his elbow to Georgiana and escorted her across the room. Fake courtship or not, they were the highest-ranking couple and he led her to the drawing room, proud to have her on his arm.

~~~~~

Hunched over her escritoire, Georgiana did not hear the door to her room open.

"I thought you'd left the schoolroom behind years ago."

She lifted her gaze to see Elizabeth at the door, dressed to go outside. At her surprised look, Lizzy said, "I did knock."

"I've been working on my next letter to Maxwell."

"So I see. You've forgotten all about your promise to go for a walk in the park with Bennet and me."

"Oh dear, is it that time already?" She sanded the portion of the letter she'd completed, which was only her salutation and stood. "Let me get my pelisse and hat. Can I meet you at the front door in ten minutes?"

"There is no rush, dearest. You can finish your letter and then we can go for our walk."

"Nonsense. Clearly you are dressed and ready. As it is, I find words escaping me at the moment."

"Anything you wish to talk about?"

"No." At Lizzy's raised eyebrow she hurried to assure her sister. "We've arrived at the letter 'Q' and I've hit a bit of a roadblock."

"Hmm… Querulous? Quarrelsome? Quirky?"

"No," Georgiana laughed. "Maxwell is none of those."

"Apologies, my quick-witted sister. I must have been projecting your quaint brother's thoughts about me."

"I appreciate your attempt to help me as you are very clever, but I think I've stumbled upon a word that suits my need."

"Do you care to share?"

"Quiet. My husband is quiet, yet in a good way."

"You know what they say about quiet people."

"Do tell."

"Still waters run deep. I'm convinced, if asked, he would take on the twelve labors of Hercules to prove his love."

Georgiana pondered Lizzy's words as they strolled the perimeter of the park, stopping at the small lake so Bennet could throw bread crumbs at the ducks. Would Maxwell perform a Herculean quest if she asked? A peace settled over heart with the knowledge that he would. Indeed, since December he'd proven over and over that he was sincere in his love and in his quest to regain her favor. It was time she moved them closer to the finish line. However, she was thoroughly enjoying their journey through the alphabet and didn't want to end their correspondence just yet.

Instead of sending a letter every third day she'd encourage him to exchange them daily. After a quick calculation, she realized they'd finish in about two weeks. She almost clapped her hands in delight. As it was the sky became bluer, the bird song more melodic and the sun shone brighter than ever.

Ten days later, after using the letter 'Y', Georgiana signed her final communication to Max. After sealing the missive, she rang for a footman to deliver it to Kerr House. Familiar with his mission, the young lad gladly walked the quarter mile before he handed it over to the butler and enjoyed his usual treat of lemon tarts.

~~~~~

Max sat behind his desk; shoulders slumped in defeat. Words refused to come to mind. They were nearing the end of the alphabet and once he received the next letter from Georgiana, he'd have to reply. A piece of ivory vellum lay beneath his hand with words written and crossed out.

~~Zephyr~~

~~Zeal~~

~~Zing~~

~~Zone~~

Zebra

He groaned. Zebra? The urge to smash his forehead against his desk nearly overwhelmed him. He absolutely refused to give up after six months of courting and exchanging letters. Instinctively he knew this was purely a symbolic gesture, but he needed to complete the task so they could begin anew. With a longsuffering sigh, he dipped his quill into the ink pot, prepared to scratch out the last word.

"A letter has arrived, your Grace."

In his despair he hadn't heard Benson open the door. He dropped the quill, unmindful of the large ink blotch created on the parchment and held out his hand. His butler handed him the single page and politely bowed out of the room.

He broke the seal and read the note. At first his heart stopped beating before thudding back to life. He pushed back his chair, nearly toppling it over in his haste to stand and call out, "Benson, my hat and cane please."

Within the half hour, he'd reached Darcy House and was admitted by the butler.

"Good afternoon, your Grace."

"Good afternoon." He handed his hat and cane to the man.

"Would you inform Miss Darcy I am here to see her?"

"Right away, sir. Would you care to wait in the blue salon?"

"Don't bother seeing me there, Hutchins. I know the way."

"Very well, your Grace. I shall return in but a moment."

Hutchins disappeared through a discreet door and Max made his way to the blue salon. He halted in the doorway when he discovered not only Darcy there, but also Ash and the Colonel.

"Adborough," Darcy acknowledged him.

He couldn't be sure, but the dour man from Derbyshire had begun to soften in his attitude, as well as his cousin, Ash. Richard, crusty old soldier that he was, refused to give in, although his muttered threats of running his through with his sword had dwindled to an occasional utterance.

All in all, things looked up for him and Georgiana.

"Gentlemen," he replied back and joined them near a grouping of chairs.

"Why are you here?"

"I've come to see Georgiana."

"You are well past receiving hours, Adborough," Richard grumbled.

"None of that, if you please, cousin." All of them swiveled their attention to the entrance. Georgiana, stunning in a deep blue gown, moved gracefully toward them. "Maxwell is family." She slanted her gaze upward to him and asked, "You received my letter?"

"I did—" He shot a look at the three men watching them. "May we have some privacy?"

"I'm not moving." Ash countered with a broad smile.

"Come with me." Georgiana slid her arm around his and they moved to the far side of the room. When she would have removed her arm from his, he captured her hand and brought it to his lips. A loud harrumphing cough from the other side of the room made him smile against her fingers. "Ignore them," she whispered. "This is between you and me."

"Did you mean what you wrote?"

"Most assuredly."

His whole body quivered and he could wait no longer. He brushed his mouth softly over hers, relishing in the way she offered her lips for more.

"I love you, Georgiana."

She melted in his arms. "And I love you," she sighed.

His mouth captured hers and he deepened the kiss. He loved her. He'd walk to Hades and back to have her in his life. He didn't care that they were standing not ten feet from her brother and cousins....

Oh, dear God, they were kissing in front of her brother and cousins!

Still cupping the sides of her face, he drew back and gazed down at her. Eyes closed, full lips slightly open, she was beautiful. Slowly, her eyes drifted open and he knew exactly when the same realization came to her. A rosy pink heated her cheeks and she grinned.

He cut a glance to the other side of the room. Darcy, Richard and Ash still stood at the door. Darcy and Richard glowered and Ash, well Ash watched the two of them with unbridled amusement.

"Gentlemen. I believe my wife and I would like some

privacy now."

"We need at least two weeks. I will let you know when you may come to Kerr house."

Max gave a start and stared down at Georgiana.

"What?" she asked, her eyes wide with unconvincing innocence. "Would you rather live here?"

"Not bloody likely." Max dropped his hands and turned toward the trio. "Three weeks, minimum," he almost growled.

"Come on.," Ash pushed off from the chair he'd been leaning against. "Our work is done here."

"Don't bother. We'll be on our way." Max began steering Georgiana toward the door.

Darcy started forward, only to be held back by Ash. "This is her choice, Darcy."

"He made her miserable. And now he's forcing her to—"

Georgiana came to a complete stop and faced her brother.

"No one is forcing me to do anything, Fitz. I love him and I belong with my husband."

"Yes, but—"

"But nothing. I know you love me, which means you must trust that I know what I'm doing."

Darcy held his sister's gaze for a moment before giving her a slight nod. He stepped forward and kissed her cheek, whispering, "You are a beautiful Duchess." He extended his hand. "Welcome to the family, Adborough."

He shook Darcy's hand and said, "Thank you."

Ash also shook his hand as he passed by and Richard stopped directly in front of them. He first looked at Georgiana, peering at her as though he needed to assure himself that she was completely serious about her decision and then he looked at Max, his expression one of resignation.

"I love you, Georgie and will abide by your wishes." He swung his gaze to Max. "One step out of line, Adborough and I will make your life a living hell."

"Richard," Georgiana chided gently. "None of us are without fault and if you've never made a wrong step, or said the wrong thing, then you can come to Max and demand perfection. Until then... mind your manners."

Clearly surprised by her words, the Colonel rocked back on his heels and assessed her again. Then he smiled. The first full one Max had seen in a long time.

"You do have the making of a formidable Duchess, cousin."

He turned smartly on his heel and followed his brother and cousin out of the room.

"Do you need some time to pack?" Max asked once he'd regained his mental equilibrium.

"I already have a few things packed." Her cheeks flushed a rosy pink. "Anna can bring the rest at a later date."

"Very well, wife," he extended his elbow. "Shall we start anew?"

As soon as they'd donned their outer wear, they walked back to Kerr house, gliding by a surprised butler and completely ignored the servants who gaped as Max carried his wife up the stairs and kicked the door to his bedroom shut.

The housekeeper was the only one who smiled knowingly as she had been the one who'd retrieved the note from Georgiana and placed it in the Duke's drawer. She hadn't meant to read the missive, but it was hard not to when there was but a single line on the whole page.

Later, Max had no memory of who made the first move. All he knew was that when the haze of desire lifted and he gazed down at his beautiful wife he noted with extreme satisfaction that her hair had fallen out of all its pins and lay in glorious curls down her back. Her lips were plump from his kisses, her cheeks flush with desire and her gown was unbuttoned in a most becoming way. His body burned at the memory of how soft her flesh felt beneath his hands and he drew her back into his embrace.

"I have one more word for you, my darling Maxwell," she murmured against his lips. "I desperately wanted to say it when I first returned to London and surprised you in the music room."

"Whatever it is, it cannot compare to what we have right now, right here," he growled with impatient desire and captured her mouth again.

They separated briefly and he rested his forehead against hers. She took the opportunity to stand on the tips of her toes and feather kisses along his jaw line, stopping when she reached the sensitive lobe of his ear. She whispered one word and with a strangled groan he gathered her into his arms and carried her to the bed before returning his attention to her mouth and body.

Minutes, days, hours passed before a sense of reason invaded his desire filled brain. He desperately wanted to consummate their marriage but needed to ensure he hadn't misread any signal she'd been sending. With much regret, he broke the kiss.

"Before we get carried away, I must ask a simple question." He expected to see a flash of disappointment, but she held his gaze with an open and honest expression. Oh, how he loved this woman. "Do you truly wish to be my wife, in *every* sense of the word?" At her nod he nearly whooped for joy.

"How can I refuse when that is also my heart's desire and has been for many years?"

The urge to draw her close and kiss her senseless almost overpowered him. Sheer will power kept his fisted hands close to his side. His thoughts and words were another matter.

"I do not deserve you. However, I would follow you to the ends of the earth and back. I never wish to be apart from you again."

"There is no need to travel to the ends of the earth," she laughed out. "The master suite here will suffice."

She gave him such a loving look his knees almost buckled. He became completely undone when she took his clenched hand in hers and after opening it wide, placed it against her soft cheek.

"Fulfill my 'I' word," she whispered into his palm. "Bring me home completely."

And he did, and for many years they expressed their *Intimate* devotion as only people truly in love can.

THE END

SueBarr.ca

www.ingramcontent.com/pod-product-compliance
Lightning Source LLC
Chambersburg PA
CBHW022201170626
46807CB00005B/2299